BLOODY VALENTINE

BLOODY VALENTINE

James Patterson
with K.A. John

SHORTLIST

First published in 2011 by
Arrow Books
This Large Print edition published
2011 by AudioGO Ltd
by arrangement with
The Random House Group Ltd

ISBN 978 1 405 62307 0

British Library Cataloguing in Publication Data available

Printed and bound in Great Britain by the MPG Books Group

CHAPTER ONE

'Killing isn't murder when it's necessary.'

The figure, dressed in black, lying on the bed, believed it. The killing that had taken so much planning would benefit more people than it would hurt. So it wouldn't be murder.

The killer listened to the faint roar of London traffic that the triple-glazed windows failed to mute, and watched the figures change on the digital clock. 2.00 a.m., 2.01 a.m., 2.03 a.m., 2.04 a.m. . . .

The click of the clock and a distant steady breathing were the only sounds apart from the traffic. The sleeping pills in the bedtime drink had worked. No one else was awake.

At 2.10 a.m. the night porter, Damian Clark, would pocket the intercom receiver. He'd leave the foyer and take his break in his studio flat in the basement. His routine hadn't varied in the six weeks that the killer had watched him.

The cameras would record, but Damian wouldn't be watching the screens above the porter's desk. It was the perfect time. With care there'd be nothing to be seen on the tapes, because the killer knew the exact angle of the cameras, where they recorded and where they didn't.

Damian's absence was an extra safety measure.

The street doors were locked. No one could enter Barnes Building without summoning Damian on the intercom and who was going to call between two and three in the morning?

No resident could enter one apartment from another unless they had the master key code. The day porter, Ted, had been stupid. When he'd been given the job three months ago, he'd written down the code and left it on a notepad on the desk.

At 2.10 a.m. the figure rose from the bed and glanced in the mirror. All that could be seen was a black shadow in the darkness. The only glimpse of colour was in the eyes shining through the slits in the ski mask. Thin latex gloves were snapped on. The pencil torch was in the trouser pocket. The bag packed.

Time to go.

The layout was the same in all the apartments except the penthouse. The front door opened into a hall. There was a kitchen on the left, a living room that opened on to a balcony straight ahead, bedrooms and bathrooms on the right. Snuffles and heavy breathing came from behind the second bedroom door. The killer listened at the outer door before opening it and creeping out into the corridor.

*   *   *

The kitchen surfaces gleamed, smelling of antiseptic, as a chef's kitchen should.

The knives were in the block. A chopper to cut through bone. A filleting knife to loosen organs. A carving knife to sever muscle. The two-pronged fork was hanging above the cooker. All were placed in the bag. Back to the hall. Listen at the door. Was it imagination, or was there a sound in the corridor?

Open the door slowly. Deep breath to steady nerves. Back into the corridor, crawling low to avoid the lens of the CCTV camera.

The building hummed with night noises. The heating whirred. The low-wattage light bulbs buzzed. Water ran in the communal utility room as a night load washed.

No one slept in the artists' studio. The plumbing under the sink was plastic, push fit. A stab with a sharp penknife split the joint. Water began to drip, enough to make a small pool by morning. It would claim the day porter's attention for an hour or two.

The stairs behind the fire doors were concrete. They led up to the penthouse roof terrace and down to the cellar car park. There were cameras trained on the outside doors. One was at the cellar car park level, another was on the roof. Nothing between.

It was easy to crawl below the red-eyed beam of the CCTV, reach up, and key in the master code. The door clicked. The killer crept forward and crawled into the secret place.

There was a light but no windows. Shelves were bolted to the walls—waist high on one side, shoulder height on the other. The secret place was small, but there was room to move around.

Chains had been wound around the shelf at waist height. Leather straps fastened to the links at measured points. Straps that would fasten ankles, knees, hips, waist, arms, wrists and neck securely to the shelf.

The killer turned to the shelves on the other side and emptied the bag except for a can of spray paint. The chef's knives and the two-pronged fork were set out in a row, steel blades gleaming in the electric light. There was a roll of red satin ribbon and a sheet of pink-heart gift wrap, a plastic box, and a white cardboard box, with a printed address label and a plastic flag. Next to them the killer laid the stun gun that looked like a mobile phone, bought in Florida and smuggled back through Gatwick. It was illegal to buy stun guns in Britain.

'Killing isn't murder when it's necessary.'

The killer spoke the words aloud. One final check before leaving, closing and locking the door. A quick spray of paint. It was a second coat. The paint was invisible, difficult to

6

check.

Back to the corridors in the building, then returning to the apartment, avoiding CCTV cameras, moving as slowly and carefully as on the journey down.

Home! The lock clicked. The sound was loud.

A cry tore through the air from behind a bedroom door. The killer froze.

CHAPTER TWO

The killer remained still, silent. The cry subsided to a soft moan. After a heart-thundering eternity, the sound of steady breathing once more echoed from behind the door.

A nightmare!

Slip into own bedroom. Undress with five minutes to spare. 3.05. Everything was ready. Close eyes, try to sleep. Tomorrow was going to be a busy day—and, for one person, their last.

*   *   *

'Happy Valentine's Day, darling.' Jack Barnes set the tray on the four-poster bed next to his wife, Zee.

She opened her eyes to a vista of pink.

'Pink rose, cranberry juice, fresh raspberries topped with raspberry yoghurt, smoked salmon and pink scrambled eggs. The eggs are a cheat. I mixed tomato juice into them.' Jack shook out the napkin and laid it over the sheet. 'The best I could do with the coffee was to serve it in a pink mug.'

'You are a sweetheart.' Zee pulled his head down and kissed him.

'The last luxury.' He uncovered a pink iced doughnut.

'If I eat that, I'll grow as big as an elephant,' Zee complained.

'In five months we'll start training

for the London Marathon so you can run off the baby weight.'

'Only if I can bear to leave the baby.'

'Strap him or her to your back,' he teased.

'Have you time for coffee?'

'No, because I'm working on another surprise.'

'What?'

'It won't be a surprise if I tell you. Enjoy breakfast. I'll meet you at the restaurant for lunch.'

'One o'clock at our usual table? Or in your office?'

'Our table. Make the most of this lazy day,' he warned. 'The next Valentine's Day will be filled with baby and nappies.'

'I'm looking forward to being a mother.'

'As opposed to wife?' he joked.

'I'll always be that.'

He went to the door and blew her a kiss. 'Love you lots.'

'Love you more.' It was her

standard reply, but it always made him smile.

*   *   *

Jack went into the living room. Their cleaner, Sara, was dusting.

'Thanks for setting up the breakfast tray, Sara.'

'My pleasure, Mr Jack. How long will you and Mrs Zee be gone?'

He held his finger to his lips. 'Zee doesn't know about the trip yet. We'll be back on Monday.'

'I'll give the apartment a good clean over the weekend.'

'It always looks immaculate to me, Sara. You do a fine job.'

'Nice of you to say so, Mr Jack.'

Jack left the apartment and, ignoring the lift, walked down the stairs. He'd lived in Barnes Buildings in Mayfair for five years. Originally two houses, he'd hired an architect to convert them into apartments for himself and his family. His penthouse was large and luxurious. It had four balconies, a roof terrace with hot tub, four en-suite bedrooms, a study, movie and games suite, formal living and dining rooms and a den.

His younger brother, Michael, lived below him and Zee, with his girlfriend Anni. As they were both artists, Jack had turned the floor below their apartment into a studio where they worked.

When Jack reached the studio floor, he saw Michael and Anni carrying one of Anni's life-sized sculptures into the lift.

'Need help?' Jack asked.

'Don't we always when Anni wants to move one of these?' Michael was breathless.

Jack took the sculpture's feet. 'What's this one stuffed with? Dead bodies or iron bars?'

'Dead body, Jack. They're easier to turn into sculptures.' Anni had an odd sense of humour.

11

'Dead body with wings. A fairy or angel?'

'Angel. It's going to my solo exhibition in the Knightsbridge gallery.'

'Zee and I are looking forward to the opening.'

'We'll take it from here, Jack.' Michael pushed the sculpture into the lift.

'The leak,' Anni reminded Michael.

Michael led Jack into the studio and showed him a pool of water under the sink. 'The pipe's split. If it's not fixed, the water will drip through on to Leila and Mamie's ceiling.'

'I'll ask the porter to see to it. If he can't sort it, he'll have to call a plumber.'

'How's Zee?' Michael asked as they walked back to the lift.

'Happy, growing. They both are.'

'Anni and I can't wait to be an aunt and uncle.'

'Fatherhood can't come soon enough for me.' Jack left them and walked down to the next floor.

The apartment on that level was occupied by his older sister Leila and his youngest sister Mamie. Leila was in her early forties, Mamie, who had Down's Syndrome, seventeen. Their front door opened when he reached the landing.

'You two look smart,' Jack complimented. 'Going somewhere special?'

'The whole school's going to the matinee of *Hamlet* in the Aldwych.' Mamie was eager to tell Jack about her outing.

'You going as well?' Jack asked Leila.

'No. I have a committee meeting.'

'Which charity?' Their parents had been killed in a car accident ten years before. Leila had given up her nursing career to care for Mamie. When Mamie left primary for secondary school, Leila had taken up charity work to fill the time that Mamie spent in school. Jack had lost count of the number of causes she supported.

'Cancer Research. We're organising a sponsored cycle ride.'

'You'll sponsor me, Jack?' Mamie asked.

'Of course,' he promised. 'So will Zee.'

'We must go, Mamie, or you'll be late.' Leila pressed the lift button. 'Is Zee over her morning sickness, Jack?'

'She hasn't thrown up for a week.'

'That's good. Have you asked if it's a boy or a girl?' Leila checked.

'No, and we won't. It'll spoil the surprise.'

Jack ran down to the next level. No sound came from the apartment. It was occupied by the senior chef he employed, Bruno Gambrini, and his partner, sous chef Adrian Wills. Bruno created recipes for Jack's chain of restaurants. Jack assumed that both of them would have been at work for hours.

The next floor housed the communal gym and swimming pool. Jack continued down the stairs and into the foyer that opened on to the street. Most of the area was taken up by a conference centre, with offices and en-suite guest rooms.

'Good morning, Mr Barnes,' the night porter greeted him.

'Day porter not on yet, Damian?' Jack looked around for Ted Levett.

Zee had been at school with Ted but had lost touch. Three months ago she'd seen him selling *The Big Issue* outside a tube station. Ted had abandoned his medical studies and was living in a hostel after his release from prison for drug dealing. He told her he'd been in rehab and was 'clean'.

Zee had persuaded Jack to employ Ted. But Jack had made it clear, even after three months of satisfactory work, that Ted was still 'on trial'.

'I'm here, Mr Barnes.' Ted appeared on the stairs that led down to the basement. 'I've been checking the chemicals in the swimming pool.'

'Are they all right?' Jack was concerned because Zee used the pool.

'Everything's fine. You can swim any time.'

'If you've nothing else to do before beginning your shift, Ted, I'm off.' Damian left the desk.

'To write another book?' Jack asked. Damian worked the night shift so he could write his science fiction and horror books in peace— although he had yet to sell one.

'Just started a new one, Mr Barnes.' Damian disappeared down the stairs leading to the basement apartments that he and Ted occupied.

'There's a leak under the sink in Michael and Anni's studio, Ted. Look at it after you've taken in the post. If you can't fix it, call a plumber.'

'Will do, Mr Barnes.'

Jack stepped outside. He loved London. The old buildings, the newspaper boys and stalls on street corners.

The twenty-minute walk to his office above his flagship restaurant in Soho was his 'thinking time'. Given the plans he was making for his romantic weekend with Zee, he was enjoying his thoughts.

Jack heard Adrian as he turned the corner. Every chef who worked for him had a voice louder than a rock star and a vile temper. He wondered if the profession attracted angry people, or if they became that way after working in hot kitchens.

He entered the restaurant. Adrian was standing outside the kitchen door, the staff crowding around him, open-mouthed, listening to his every word.

CHAPTER THREE

Adrian was an excellent mimic and sounded more like Bruno than Bruno. 'I'll follow you in ten minutes,' Adrian boomed in Bruno's voice before reverting to his own. 'That's what Bruno said when I left the apartment. Ten minutes! That was three hours ago. Bruno was lying in bed then and I bet that's where Bruno is now. Leaving me to do all the work.'

'You have a problem, Adrian?' Jack asked.

'I have a big problem, Mr Barnes. His name is Bruno. He wouldn't get out of bed this morning.'

Jack looked at the junior chefs and waitresses. 'All of you, back to work,' he ordered. They walked away, but Jack knew from the silence that they were still listening.

'Is Bruno ill?' Jack asked.

'He complained he had a headache. I gave him two aspirin and he said he'd follow me. But . . .' Adrian flung his arms wide. 'Where is he?'

'Bruno doesn't often have headaches,' Jack commented. 'I'll phone the apartment and check he's all right.'

'There's no point,' Adrian argued. 'He's not answering the telephone and he's switched off his mobile. He never gets up when he has a brandy headache.'

'A brandy headache?' Jack repeated. 'Bruno was drunk last night?'

'He was.'

'Bruno doesn't drink on work nights.'

'Not usually,' Adrian confirmed. 'But someone sent him a bottle yesterday.'

'Who?'

'The note was signed, "Grateful customer". It was sent to the kitchen before we closed. I knew there'd be trouble when Bruno took it home. I supervised the cleaning here. When I got back to Barnes Building, Bruno was watching TV and the bottle was half empty. I went to bed. When I got up this morning, I looked for the bottle and there was only this much—' Adrian put his finger and thumb close together 'left in the bottom. After what Bruno drank, he won't want to get up this afternoon, this evening, or tomorrow morning either.'

'I'll leave a message on his voicemail and send a messenger to make sure it's only a hangover,' Jack said. 'Can you cope? Or should I send for agency staff?'

Adrian tossed his head in the air. 'Agency staff can't tell a carrot from an onion, and I've yet to work with one who can boil an egg. I'll just have to cope.'

Jack knew better than to contradict a chef. 'If you need help, see me. I'll be in the office all morning.'

'You won't forget to send a messenger to Bruno, Mr Barnes?'

'I won't.' Jack pressed the lift button.

* * *

Jack's main office was on the top floor of the block and as expensively furnished as his penthouse.

'Happy Valentine's Day,' Jack's secretary, Alice, greeted him when he walked into reception. 'Your messages are on your desk with the letters you need to sign. I've called up your e-mails. They're on screen. Would you like coffee?'

'Please, Alice. Then get me the chauffeur-driven limousine firm we use and the hotel in Helford Creek I've booked.'

'If you want to arrange champagne and truffles in the car and flowers, champagne and a fruit basket in your hotel suite, I've done it.'

Jack smiled. 'What would I do without you?'

'Hire another girl to make your calls. I'm only sorry I can't control the chefs.'

'You heard Adrian?'

'I tried not to, but he was too loud. All the chefs are stressed, which isn't surprising on Valentine's Day. A fight broke out in the kitchen of the Edinburgh restaurant. I confirmed everything's back to what passes for normal there half an hour ago. The good news is there's not a table to be had in a Barnes' restaurant tonight in Britain.'

'That's what I like to hear: fully booked.' Jack opened his office door.

'The butchers have an appointment to see you in an hour about the meat order.'

'Show them straight in and send a messenger over to Bruno's apartment with a note telling him to get in here, please. Or, if he can't, to telephone me.'

'Anything else, Jack?'

'Make sure no one's double-booked my table downstairs. Zee and I will lunch at one.'

'Your coffee.' Alice poured him a cup from the filter machine, black and strong with three brown sugars, the way he liked it.

Jack took the mug, went into his office, closed the door and walked to the window. He looked out and admired the view, as he did every working day.

There wasn't another city like London in the world. And as long as Zee remained by his side, there wasn't a single thing he'd change in his life.

The telephone rang. Jack picked it up.

The voice was low, almost a whisper. It took a moment for Jack to recognise it as Bruno's.

'I'm dying, Jack. Help me.'

CHAPTER FOUR

Zee ate her breakfast before running a bath. She soaked in lemon-scented bath oil while reading a magazine, enjoying every lazy moment.

When she'd met Jack she'd been a waitress in one of his restaurants. Before leaving drama school she'd dreamed of becoming a model or an actress. But the training hadn't equipped her for the competition at auditions, or the loss of confidence she experienced after every rejection.

She'd fallen in love with Jack at first sight. She knew he was attracted to her, but when she'd met his family, they'd been suspicious of her. There was a fifteen-year age gap between her and Jack; she was poor and he was rich. Leila believed Zee was after Jack's money and told her so. Michael was convinced Jack had married her because he couldn't bear living alone after the unexpected death of his first wife, four months before Zee and Jack had started dating.

Zee couldn't ignore Michael and Leila's comments. She hoped the baby she was carrying would convince Jack's family it was the man she loved, not the lifestyle and presents he gave her.

She left the bath, dried herself and dressed in one of the maternity suits she'd bought in Harrods. She straightened her hair, applied make-up, sprayed Jack's favourite perfume on to her neck and wrists and left her bedroom.

'Good morning, Mrs Zee, you look lovely,' Sara complimented.

'Thank you, Sara.' Zee noticed an arrangement of red roses.

'Six dozen, Mrs Zee. They arrived ten minutes ago. From Mr Jack.' Sara handed her a package and envelope. 'These came with them.'

Zee opened the letter first. She

smiled. 'It's a booking for three nights starting tonight, in our favourite hotel in Cornwall.'

'And the parcel,' Sara reminded.

Zee opened it. 'Silk underwear. I'd better pack.'

'Lay everything you want to take on the sofa in your bedroom. I'll pack it in your weekend luggage.'

'You're an angel, Sara.' Zee pulled a rosebud from the arrangement and handed it to the maid.

'Thank you, Mrs Zee. I'll show it to my boyfriend and hope it will make him jealous enough to ask me to marry him.'

Zee went into the bedroom and laid out a selection of her own and Jack's casual clothes. On the way out of the apartment, she pulled eight more roses from the display and wrapped each in a tissue.

'You have other loves besides Mr Jack, Mrs Zee?' Sara sprayed polish on the floor.

'Hoping to make people happy.'

26

Zee removed one more rosebud. Jack's secretary, Alice, had been the only person in Jack's life who'd approved of their marriage. Zee laid the roses inside her handbag, checked her reflection in the mirror, and went to the door. 'Thank you, Sara. Jack will send someone to pick up the cases. I'll see you on Monday.'

'Enjoy your break, Mrs Zee. You're leaving early for lunch.'

'I'll do some baby shopping on the way.' Zee was too proud to admit she hoped Jack's brother or sister would invite her in for coffee before she left the apartment block. She needed to convince them that she loved Jack and was looking forward to becoming the mother of his child. The first of many she and Jack had planned.

*　　　*　　　*

Zee took the lift to the next floor and knocked at Michael and Anni's apartment. When there was no reply, she walked down to the artists' studio. It was locked. She left two roses and the Valentine cards she'd written for Michael and Anni outside the door.

She heard music coming from Leila and Mamie's apartment, but no one answered her knock. Suspecting Leila was avoiding her, she left rosebuds and cards there as well.

She didn't knock on Bruno and Adrian's door because she assumed they'd be in the restaurant. She left flowers and cards for them too and took the lift to reception. Ted the porter looked up from the desk when she entered the foyer.

'I've been watching you on CCTV. All I can say, after you've made everyone else's Valentine's Day special, is: Happy Valentine's Day, Zee.'

Zee gave him his card and rose. 'I've a card and rose for Damian as well.' She took them from her bag and left them on the desk.

'I'll give them to him when we change shift. It's more than my life's worth to disturb him when he's writing or sleeping. Enjoy your day.'

'I will.' Zee smiled at the thought of going to Cornwall. They chatted for another few minutes, then Zee looked at her watch. 'I'd better get on, Ted,' she said, smiling a farewell.

'Button your coat,' he warned. 'The sun may be shining but it's freezing out there.'

She took Ted's advice, wrapped her scarf around her neck and walked out of the door.

Zee checked her watch. She wanted to buy an extra present for Jack. Something he'd use every day. A wallet? A key ring? One he could slip a photograph of their baby into, after he or she was born.

The heart-shaped gold cufflinks she'd wrapped were nothing compared to the roses and romantic weekend Jack had planned. She knew from experience that when Jack organised a surprise for her, it was perfect to the last detail.

She turned right, towards the shops. A van was parked outside the florist's. A young man was filling buckets with blooms. She stopped to admire a display of red and gold roses.

The side door of the van slid back. She heard her name. She turned and stared in surprise.

'Hello. What are you doing in there dressed like that?'

There was an answering smile. 'Climb inside and you'll find out.'

Zee stepped in. The door slammed behind her. Suddenly afraid, Zee shivered.

CHAPTER FIVE

Jack's telephone rang. He picked it up.

'It's the doctor you asked to call on Bruno, Jack,' Alice announced.

'Put him through.'

'Jack?'

'Peter, how are you?'

'Fine. And so's your chef.'

'Bruno's not dying?'

'A couple of days' rest and he'll be back to normal. I've given him a leaflet on alcohol abuse and left a couple of aspirins for his headache.'

'Thanks, Peter. I owe you one.'

'Next round of golf at the club is on you. Wednesday at three?'

'I'll be there.'

'Do you want to speak to Bruno?'

'Not until Monday. I intend to enjoy my weekend.' Jack replaced the receiver and saw Alice watching him. 'Save me from overdramatic chefs.'

'Is there any other kind?' Alice returned to her own desk.

*   *   *

Lamplight flooded the back of the van.

'Stand back, Zee. I don't want anyone to see what I'm about to show you.'

'You're being very mysterious.' Zee forced a smile. It was ridiculous to be afraid of someone she knew so well.

The light was strong. Zee blinked, opened her eyes, and saw it.

Black, larger than a mobile phone, it touched her shoulder and she instantly felt weak. Too sick to move or think. She slumped to the metal floor. Her muscles hardened to stone. All she could think about was her baby.

Zee opened her mouth to scream but her lips refused to part. The pain

32

was so intense that the cry she'd intended was a weak groan. Hands closed around her neck. She tumbled headfirst into darkness.

* * *

Zee struggled to open her eyes. Or, rather, she thought she had, but she couldn't be certain. Everything was black. She was aware of agonising pain in every muscle. Pain that prevented her from moving. Was she having a nightmare?

She tried to lift her arms and failed. Then she realised that they, like her legs, neck and head, were fastened to a cold, hard surface. There was a foul taste in her mouth. Something had been pushed between her teeth. Something dry, hard and nasty. No matter how she tried to push it aside with her tongue, she couldn't.

She'd never been afraid of the dark. Now she was. There was a buzzing. A sense of movement.

Zee remembered stopping on the pavement. Entering the van. The door closing. The noise—was it the engine of the van? Was she being taken somewhere? Had she been kidnapped?

The buzzing stopped. There was stillness and silence.

What could have been one or five minutes later, metal slammed against metal. The sound sent shivers crawling down her spine. Footsteps drew nearer . . . The side door opened. She'd heard the driver's door of the van closing.

Someone stepped inside the back of the van. The door closed. A light was switched on. It burned her eyes. She closed them tightly.

'A little pain. The last, I promise. Then it will stop hurting.' The voice was soft, kind. But Zee was terrified. Not for herself. Her baby . . . Jack . . . She fought against the straps that pinned her down. She couldn't move more than a fraction of an inch.

Bracing herself for the pain of the light, she forced her eyes open. A black figure leaned over her. A cap covered the hair, a mask the face. All she could see was the eyes. Dark and glittering.

Light reflected from hands that were covered in white latex. She saw a blade. She made one last effort . . .

Too late. The edge of the chopper sliced through her jacket and continued plunging downwards. She felt warm, wet blood gush from her chest, soaking her skin.

Then she heard it. Metal scraping bone. The pain got worse.

She gasped for breath. She couldn't breathe. She heard a loud crack . . . followed by another . . . and another . . .

CHAPTER SIX

It came to Zee in a burst of sickening knowledge. The cracks were her ribs breaking one by one. Then one crack, louder than all the others, brought a pain too great to bear.

The killer stood over Zee. The straps only allowed small movements, but that didn't stop Zee fighting. Slowly, so slowly that the killer couldn't be certain it was really happening, Zee's eyes dulled. Gradually, they lost the brightness of life. Zee's eyelids flickered but they did not close. A bubble of pink froth escaped from her mouth. Blood welled from her opened chest, staining her cream jacket crimson.

Zee sighed. A last sigh. Her eyes opened wide.

They were blind and dead.

The killer looked from Zee's face to the opening in her chest. The handle of the chopping knife stuck out. The killer thrust it down and turned it, pushing Zee's broken ribs apart. A loud 'snap' startled the killer, who listened for an outside noise.

There was none.

Working quickly, the killer pushed aside the ragged remains of clothing and freed Zee's ribs from her breast plate until a gap was exposed in her chest. The chopper was exchanged for the filleting knife. A few delicate probing movements exposed Zee's heart.

Holding the carving knife in one hand, the filleting knife in the other, the killer cut through the blood vessels and tissue that held the heart in place. The filleting knife had a fine blade. The carving knife was sharp. It took only two minutes to prise Zee's heart free.

Changing the latex gloves for a clean pair, the killer picked up the two-pronged fork and speared Zee's heart. A few seconds later it was in the plastic box. It proved difficult to scratch the initials on to the surface. The knives were sharp but the heart was slippery. Eventually the letters could be read—just.

The flag was already prepared. The printed note was secured to the top. The killer jabbed it into the heart and changed gloves before closing the lid on the plastic box.

A swift examination confirmed there was no blood on the outside of the container.

Changing gloves yet again, the clean plastic box was placed in the centre of the sheet of wrapping paper. The killer tucked in the ends of paper and secured it around the plastic box with the red ribbon, tying the ends into a neat bow.

When the plastic box was wrapped, it was placed inside the cardboard box. Then the lid was closed and fastened. The pre-printed address label was placed on top.

The box was left on the end of the shelf, away from the bloodied knives.

Clean-up time. The killer had entered the secret place fully clothed. Hair had always been covered. Fibres may have been shed but, once the clothes had been burned in the incinerator, there would be nothing for the police to match the fibres to.

There were no fingerprints, only smudges from the latex gloves.

The floor was sticky with blood. There were footprints, but the rubber-soled shoes would also be placed in the incinerator. And the killer had taken the precaution of buying footwear two sizes too large.

The bloodied knives were packed into the plastic bag that had been used to carry them into the van. The gloves went into another clean plastic bag along with the stun gun, scissors, leftover ribbon and wrapping paper. Zee's handbag lay on the floor where she'd dropped it.

The killer opened it, switched off the mobile phone and left it. There was another bag in the corner. One that held clean clothes.

It was cold in the van. It would be colder outside. The killer opened the van cautiously. No one was about. Before leaving the van the bloody-soled shoes were removed and packed into a clean bag. Then the killer locked the van door and moved swiftly to the incinerator room. There was no CCTV there.

The killer stripped off, removed mask, socks, clothes and under-clothes, and placed them in the bag with the shoes. All the contents of that bag were pushed into the flames followed by the leftover ribbon, scissors, wrapping paper, gloves and van keys. The last object burned was the stun gun. The knives were still needed. Dressed in street clothes and wearing a clean pair of gloves, the killer left the room and climbed the stairs once more. There was no CCTV on the basement floor that housed the porters' studio apartments either.

There was the sound of music. Damian was awake and writing.

The killer used the master key code to enter Ted's apartment. A dirty shirt was in the linen basket in the bathroom. The killer wiped the bloody knives and fork on the shirt but was careful to leave a little blood on the blades. The knives were replaced in the bag. Just as the killer was placing the shirt at the bottom of the basket and piling the rest of the dirty linen on top, the sound of key code buttons being pressed was followed by the door opening.

CHAPTER SEVEN

There was no time to close the bathroom door. The killer stepped behind it and watched the studio through the crack.

Damian was in the kitchen area. He opened a cupboard, took out a jar of coffee, scribbled a note on a pad and left. The door closed behind him.

The killer let out a deep breath, then, crept from the bathroom and read the note.

RAN OUT OF COFFEE. TOOK YOURS. WILL REPLACE, DAMIAN.

The killer listened at the door before creeping out of Ted's apartment. All was quiet.

*   *   *

There was a glass panel in the door that opened from the back stairs into the foyer. The CCTV screens were playing to an empty room. As planned, Ted was working on the plumbing in the studio. A minute to place the box with its printed message on the porter's desk.

URGENT DELIVERY FOR
MR JACK BARNES TO BE
SENT IMMEDIATELY

Up two flights of stairs, avoiding the cameras. Use the key code. Enter the apartment. Close the door.

'What the hell . . . ?'

Bruno was in the hall.

No time to think. The killer pulled one of the knives from the bag and stabbed him.

CHAPTER EIGHT

'Urgent delivery for Mr Barnes.' The messenger, with his motorbike helmet under his arm, dropped a cardboard box on to Alice's desk. He handed her an electronic pad.

Alice scribbled her signature. 'I

never get this right. It looks as though a spider has crawled across the glass.'

'Beats me how they read them,' the courier agreed. 'See you.'

Alice picked up the box and glanced at the clock. The meat suppliers had been in with Jack for an hour, which was the time limit he set on business meetings. She knocked on his door.

'Come in.' Jack was standing shaking hands with his visitors.

'You won't regret increasing your order, Mr Barnes.'

'I hope I won't. Alice, would you see my visitors out please?'

'This way,' Alice smiled at them before ushering them out of Jack's office.

Jack saw the parcel Alice had left on his desk. He'd seen a small box in a Harrod's bag in Zee's handbag when she'd left it open, but he'd thought she'd give him her Valentine gift at lunch.

He took a pair of scissors from his desk drawer and cut through the strip that fastened the box. Inside was a beautifully wrapped package.

'It's a shame to untie that bow.' Alice was in the open doorway.

'Zee's good at presentation,' Jack commented.

'It's wonderful to see two people so in love.'

'Enough of your teasing, Alice.'

'I wasn't teasing. Just jealous.' She waited while Jack cut through the ribbon.

'This is like the children's game, pass the parcel.' Jack removed the heart-strewn wrapping paper to reveal a plastic box.

'Zee's making sure you receive whatever it is in one piece.'

Jack prised the lid from the box. His eyes widened. He stepped back and crashed into the wall.

Alice moved closer, turned pale and retched.

CHAPTER NINE

Jack read the label on the bloody lump of flesh in the box.

ZEE BROKE MY HEART SO
I TOOK HERS. BUT YOUR
NAME WAS ON IT. YOU
CAN KEEP IT.

The initials JB were scratched into the muscle below the flag.

'I'll phone the police.' Alice picked up the receiver.

'No,' Jack whispered hoarsely. 'Not until after you've phoned Zee.'

*   *   *

Sergeant Ben Miller tossed the Valentine card that Inspector Amy Stuart had given him aside. 'Valentines are supposed to be secret, not handed over in person.'

46

'Given the way you avoid people, especially women people, were you expecting a card from a secret admirer?' Amy demanded.

'I lead a full private life.'

Amy looked Ben in the eye. 'You do?'

'I do,' he repeated. 'And, what's this?' He held up a voucher folded into the card. 'What's a one-legged man supposed to do with six free sessions in the gym?'

'Get fit,' Amy suggested through a mouthful of hot dog.

'Like you?' Ben mocked. 'I've never known a woman eat so much junk food.'

'That's why I go to the gym every morning. To work off the calories. Dare you to meet me there at six o'clock tomorrow morning?' she asked.

'The way you two argue, anyone would think you've been married for years.' Superintendent Davies joined them at their desks.

'Try uncle and niece,' Ben corrected.

Amy's father had worked with Ben Miller for fifteen years. The car crash that had cost Ben Miller his leg had killed Amy's father. Ben had taken a year to recover. When he'd returned to the force, he'd had to fight to remain on active service. Amy had fought alongside him, arguing that Ben's brains weren't affected by his missing limb.

'More like annoying interfering uncle and despairing niece, ma'am. You have a case for us?' Amy pushed the last of her hot dog into her mouth.

'A case, or a sick practical joke,' Barbara Davies answered. 'Someone sent Jack Barnes a heart.'

Amy wiped her hands on a tissue. 'Jack Barnes. The restaurant owner Jack Barnes?' Jack Barnes wasn't only an entrepreneur and owner of a chain of restaurants. He was a popular celebrity who 'guested' on

TV shows. Amy had seen him several times. He was always witty, amusing and well informed about whatever topic was being discussed.

'That Jack Barnes,' Barbara confirmed.

'It's Valentine's Day,' Ben pointed out.

'The heart's real.'

'Human or animal?'

'The lab's checking. The message that came with it suggested it belonged to Jack's wife Zee. Her mobile's switched off. The last signal came from the apartment building they live in.'

'How do you want to proceed, ma'am?' Amy reached for her notebook.

'I've sent Sergeant Reece and a team to Barnes Building. Jack and Zee Barnes live in the penthouse. Sergeant Reece has orders to interview the residents and begin a search. He'll report to you. I suggest you begin by interviewing Mr

Barnes.'

'We're on our way.' Amy grabbed her bag.

'Jack Barnes is high profile. The tabloids will make this front page, so avoid journalists. Here's what little paperwork I have.' Barbara handed Amy a thin file.

*   *   *

'Inspector Amy Stuart and Sergeant Ben Miller to see you, sir.' Alice showed them into Jack's office.

Jack was at his desk but he'd turned his chair to the window. His face was grey, his eyes unnaturally bright.

Amy spoke first. 'I'm sorry, Mr Barnes, we've no news. We were only assigned to the case twenty minutes ago.'

'Zee . . . my wife . . .'

'Officers are searching for her,' Ben assured him.

Jack glanced at his watch. 'The

50

parcel arrived three-quarters of an hour ago. I wanted to go to the apartment but the porter said she'd left the building ... We were meeting here for lunch. Her phone's switched off. She never switches it off ...'

'Are there any friends she might have visited?' Amy interrupted.

'My brother and sisters live in the building. The porter said Zee left around twenty past eleven. I feel so useless. The heart? The constable took it away for tests ...'

'We haven't had the results yet, sir.' Amy changed the subject. 'What about shops? Are there any between your apartment and here that your wife might have visited?'

'Dozens.' Jack looked at his watch again. 'But it's ten to one. Even if she went shopping, she'd be here by now. We lunch at one o'clock and she's always early.' He stared at the tiny figures walking on the street below. 'I don't know what to do ...'

'We agreed it would be best for

you to wait here, Jack,' Alice said softly.

'The officer who took the heart said it could be just a sick joke. He thought it could be the heart of a pig or a sheep?' The look in Jack's eyes said what he couldn't put into words. He wanted it to be a hoax.

Amy's mobile rang. She answered it.

'Sergeant Reece here, ma'am. We've found a body in Barnes Building. The murderer was next to it. Holding a knife.'

CHAPTER TEN

'I've been expecting you two.' Patrick O'Kelly, the most eccentric of the Home Office pathologists who worked with the police was drinking coffee from a specimen beaker. A heart was on a slab in front of him.

'This is a quick stop. Sergeant

Reece found a body in Barnes Building and a man next to it holding a knife.'

'The body—'

'Has a heart.' Amy referred to the notes Barbara had given her and looked around. There was no sign of the box the heart had been packed in, or the wrapping.

'Is this heart human?' Ben asked.

'Without a doubt.' Patrick pulled off his gloves, opened a body drawer in the bank behind him and removed a packet of biscuits.

'Fresh?' Amy asked.

'Yes.'

'How fresh?' Amy pressed.

'On the basis of the blood in the arteries, I'd say it was taken from the body of an adult less than an hour before Jack Barnes received it. It's the heart of a young person. There's no sign of disease or aging. Biscuit?' He thrust the packet of chocolate digestives at Amy.

'No thank you.'

Patrick offered them to Ben, who shook his head.

'Coffee? Tea? Jenny can rinse out a couple of specimen beakers.'

'We had a large breakfast.' Amy knew Patrick tried to shock officers by drinking coffee out of beakers used to store body parts. She'd never asked, but hoped he kept a separate set for his and his assistants' use.

Patrick bit into his biscuit. 'The blood group matches that of the missing woman.'

'That was quick work.' Amy was surprised.

'Jack Barnes's secretary had Jack and Zee Barnes's medical records on file. They honeymooned on safari in Africa. Jack carried a medical kit in case either of them became ill or injured.'

'What kind of medical kit?' Amy asked.

'Syringes, antibiotics, bags of saline solution, over-the-counter medicines. Nothing suspicious.'

'Have the boxes the heart was delivered in been examined?'

'Being examined now. The outer cardboard box had four sets of prints. The lab's working on them. But I'm guessing they belong to the porter at Barnes Building, the motorbike messenger, Jack Barnes's secretary, and Jack Barnes. The inside box, wrapping paper and ribbon had smudges overlaid by Jack Barnes's prints.'

'Latex gloves,' Ben suggested.

'Probably.' Patrick finished his biscuit and took another.

'What about DNA and tissue match?' Amy persisted.

'A constable delivered Mrs Barnes's toothbrush to us. A technician is working on her DNA profile. Another is looking at the inside and outside of the boxes. But don't expect a forensic miracle. Whoever did this knows how we work.'

'Sick bastard,' Ben murmured.

'I agree,' Patrick concurred. 'Whether it's real or a hoax, it would take a diseased mind to think up this one. Did you know she was pregnant?'

'How many months?' Amy questioned.

Patrick finished his coffee. 'The baby's not the motive. Zee Barnes was five months pregnant. The foetus wouldn't be viable.'

'So if this heart is Zee Barnes's, we're looking for a double murderer?' Ben suggested.

'If you consider a five-month foetus a human being, yes.' Patrick pulled up his mask.

Ben studied the heart. 'I'm no expert, but that looks like a neat removal to me.'

'It's not bad,' Patrick agreed.

'The work of a doctor?' Amy questioned.

Patrick walked to the slab. 'If it was, the doctor didn't use medical instruments.' He picked up the end of an artery with forceps. 'See the jagged edge? This was cut several times by a large blade, not delicately by a scalpel. The removal wasn't the result of fine surgery. Whoever took this heart from the body used knives.'

'Any particular knives?' Amy asked.

Patrick prodded the centre of the heart. 'Here we have two puncture wounds about one inch apart. The tissue around the wounds is stretched. Possibly caused when the heart was lifted from the body.'

'By a fork?' Amy looked at Patrick.

'A two-pronged domestic carving fork comes to mind.'

Amy shuddered. 'You're saying this heart was removed from a human body using a butcher's carving knife and fork?'

'Not a butcher's,' Patrick corrected. 'Butchers' knives are larger than kitchen knives. There's also the initials. Not very clear, but

I'd say some effort was put into carving them with a knife with a serrated edge.'

'JB,' Ben read.

'Jack Barnes. Fits with the message on the flag.' Amy tried to recall it word for word.

' "Zee broke my heart so I took hers but your name was on it. You can keep it",' Patrick quoted.

'If that heart was Zee Barnes's, we have work to do,' Ben prompted Amy.

'You have work to do whether it is or isn't Zee Barnes's,' Patrick pointed out. 'This heart was taken from a live body less than two hours ago. If the person concerned was sane, I doubt they consented.'

'You're certain the person was alive when the heart was removed?' Amy tried to remain professional, but the thought horrified her.

'The arteries were cut while blood was pumping through them.'

'Was the victim unconscious?'

'We've picked up no trace of anaesthetics or sedatives in the blood. But we're still running tests.'

'Is there anything else you can tell us?' Ben looked at his watch.

'The heart was removed from the body by someone with a basic knowledge of anatomy.'

'Doctor, nurse?' Amy asked.

'Butcher or chef, someone used to cutting up animal carcasses. Almost anyone with a reasonable knowledge of human anatomy. So you can include artists, keep-fit instructors, hospital technicians . . .'

'In short, about half the population,' Ben complained.

'I'm a pathologist, not a fortune-teller. I can only examine evidence,' Patrick lectured.

'You have our mobile numbers?' Amy checked.

'I do. I'll be able to tell you more if you send me the corpse the heart was taken from.'

'We'll do our best.'

*   *   *

A technician handed Amy, Ben and Sergeant Reece protective clothing as they entered the foyer of Barnes Building. They covered themselves in the white suits, bonnets and overshoes before snapping on gloves.

Constable Michelle Green was waiting for Amy and Ben at the desk. 'Sergeant Reece is with the suspect, ma'am. He was found in the apartment on the second floor.'

'He's still there?'

'Yes, ma'am. The doctor's with him. Sergeant Reece is waiting for you. Lift straight ahead of you. Only one of the four is operational. Forensic are working in the others.'

'Has the suspect been identified?'

'All I know is that he's a resident, ma'am.'

CHAPTER ELEVEN

The lift was covered in fine grey fingerprint powder. White-suited technicians were swarming over the corridor. A suited constable was standing guard outside the apartment door.

'Ma'am, sir. The duty pathologist is examining the corpse. I've been ordered to warn you to step inside carefully.' He opened the door for them.

A woman rose from the floor where she'd been kneeling beside the body.

'Preliminary report?' Amy was abrupt, shaken by the size of the pool of blood standing proud around the corpse.

Sergeant Reece left the bedroom. 'Ma'am, sir. The porter has identified the victim as Bruno Gambrini. He occupied this apartment with his partner, Adrian Wills. Both are chefs who work for Jack Barnes. Mr Wills, who was also identified by the porter, was found slumped over Mr Gambrini's corpse. He was holding a carving knife and his clothes are stained with Mr Gambrini's blood.'

The pathologist took over. 'Serrations on the knife match the wounds in Mr Gambrini's abdomen and neck. Rigor mortis hasn't set in, so death was within the last three hours. There are two stab wounds. One to the abdomen, one to the neck. The one to the neck severed the jugular before hitting the spine. There are bone fragments on the knife and at the entry point of the wound, which were probably left when the knife was withdrawn. Mr Gambrini died from blood loss, probably within a minute of his jugular being severed. No organs have been removed.' The pathologist called to the technicians. 'You can move the body out now.'

'You'll notify me of the post mortem results?'

'You should have them by the end of the day, ma'am.'

*   *   *

Sergeant Reece stood back. 'The suspect is in the bedroom, ma'am, sir.'

Amy and Ben picked their way around the corpse and pools of blood and entered the bedroom. A man in bloodied chefs' whites, his hands and feet bagged in plastic, was sitting, slumped, on his bed. He was holding his head and moaning. The police doctor was checking his blood pressure.

'Mr Wills?'

The man lifted his head and stared at Amy, She could see from the vacant expression in his eyes that he was in shock. The police doctor shook his head, warning Amy off

63

trying to question his patient.

Amy motioned to Sergeant Reece and Ben. They left the room and entered the living room, where three forensic technicians were working.

'As soon as the doctor's finished with Mr Wills, get him to the station. Search him, send hand and nail swabs and all his clothes to the laboratory.'

'Yes, ma'am.'

'Let me know when he's fit for questioning.'

'Yes, ma'am. We checked with the porter. Mr Wills entered the foyer at ten minutes to one. Constable Bradley found him here, with the corpse, at two minutes to one.'

'Eight minutes,' Amy mused.

'Less,' Ben observed. 'It would have taken at least two minutes to get here from the foyer.'

'Anything else?' Amy asked.

'Yes, ma'am. We found two bloodstained knives and a fork in the sink. I sent them to the lab.'

'Fingerprints?' Amy asked.

'So far only Bruno Gambrini's and Adrian Wills's, overlaid by smudges, probably from latex gloves.'

'I suspect that's all we're going to find.'

'I've ordered an incident room to be set up in the conference centre on the ground floor. The porter told us it's been locked since it was cleaned two days ago.'

'Thank you, Sergeant Reece. If you need us, contact us there.'

*　　　*　　　*

Michelle Green updated Ben and Amy when they entered the conference centre. 'No trace of Mrs Barnes has been found as yet, ma'am. This is a list of people living in the building, and, this is a copy of the statement I took from the day porter, Ted Levett.' Michelle handed Amy two sheets of paper. 'He confirmed Mrs Barnes left the building at 11.20 a.m. No one has seen her since. Officers are examining the CCTV tapes for the past twenty-four hours.' Michelle pointed to a bank of computers set against the wall.

'Have you told the doorman why we're looking for Mrs Barnes?'

'No, ma'am. Sergeant Reece said to keep it quiet.'

'Has the area around the building been searched?' Ben questioned.

'Organised searches inside and outside the building are ongoing, sir. Sergeant Reece has placed officers at all entrances and exits. We've orders to hold anyone entering or leaving, until they, and their business have been checked out by him. Yourselves excepted, of course, ma'am, sir.'

'How many entrances are there?' Ben asked.

'Four, sir. The foyer. A fire exit that opens into a closed yard at the back and vehicle and pedestrian access out of the underground garage.'

Ben looked at Amy. 'Start with the porter?'

She nodded. They returned to the foyer and approached the desk. 'I'm Inspector Amy Stuart, and this is Sergeant Miller.'

'I've told the constable all I know, and signed a statement.' Ted's hands were shaking.

'How long have you worked here, Mr Levett?'

'Three months. Mrs Barnes got me the job. We were at school together.'

'Do I know you, Mr Levett?' Ben leaned on the desk.

Ted avoided looking at Ben. 'Yes, officer. I went down for drug dealing?'

'Really, Mr Levett?' Ben queried. 'I remember the charge as murder.'

CHAPTER TWELVE

'The charge was reduced to manslaughter,' Ted protested. 'I'm not proud of being a pusher. I only sold enough to finance my own habit. I didn't know the "China"—'

'You mean heroin?' Amy interrupted.

'Yes. I thought it was pure. I really did. I sold it on in good faith. Look, I admit, when I was hooked I'd steal anything I could lay my hands on to buy a fix, even my suppliers' stash.'

'And your supplier had poisoned his stash,' Ben said.

'I thought it was good. Honest to God, I really thought it was OK. I would never have sold it otherwise. I got five years, came out in two and came out clean. Been clean ever since.' Ted wasn't looking for sympathy. Neither was Ben about to give him any.

'When were you released?' Ben watched the screens above the desk. All were connected to CCTV cameras inside the building.

'A year ago. My family didn't want to know me. I slept rough before I found a place in a hostel. Zee . . . Mrs Barnes, saw me selling *The Big Issue*. She got me this job and the flat that goes with it. I've a lot to be grateful to her for. If something's happened to her—'

'What makes you think something's happened to her?' Ben interrupted.

'Police officers searching the building.'

'Bruno Gambrini's been murdered,' Ben pointed out.

'He and Adrian were always quarrelling and threatening to kill one another.'

'You don't seem particularly upset,' Amy looked at him.

'I hardly knew them. They usually leave the building before I come on shift and arrive back after I've finished for the day. I doubt I've exchanged more than a couple of words with them in the three months I've been here.'

'Did you hear them quarrelling after Adrian arrived at ten to one today?'

Ted thought for a moment. 'No, but if the apartment door was closed, I wouldn't have. Constable Green was already here and taking my statement. She asked me what time Mrs Barnes left this morning. Mrs Barnes's mobile is switching straight to answerphone. I've never known her to turn it off. Something must have happened to her. Please tell me what it is?'

Amy remained cool, professional. 'Is anyone in Mr and Mrs Barnes's apartment?'

'No, Sara left shortly after Mrs Barnes. She's their cleaner.'

'How soon after Mrs Barnes left?'

'About half an hour.'

'Did Mr and Mrs Barnes know you had a record when they employed you?' Ben probed.

'I told Zee the day she saw me selling *The Big Issue*. When she persuaded Mr Barnes to meet me, I told him exactly what I'd done. I thought it only fair he knew who he was employing and inviting to live in the building.'

Amy studied the list of residents. 'How many people are in the building now?'

'The penthouse is empty. Mr Michael Barnes and his girlfriend Miss Anni Jones came in shortly after Sergeant Reece and the police constables arrived. Their apartment is below Mr and Mrs Barnes's. The next floor down is Michael Barnes's and Miss Jones's studio—they're artists. The misses Leila and Mamie Barnes, Mr Barnes's sisters, occupy the apartment on the third floor. Mamie's in a special school; she has Down's syndrome. Miss Leila is at

71

one of her charity committee meetings. Then there are the chefs. The next floor down, the one above this, is the communal gym and swimming pool. As you see,' Ted indicated a screen above the desk, 'no one's using it at present.'

'What time did Leila Barnes leave?' Amy took her notebook from her pocket.

'About twenty to one. She told me about the committee meeting on her way out.'

'You chat to the residents?' Ben continued to monitor the screens above the desk.

'We exchange friendly words. They're nice people.' Ted pointed to the roses in a glass on his desk. 'Mrs Barnes gave me those. She left roses and Valentine cards for everyone outside their doors before she went out.'

'She gave you two?' Ben smelled them.

'One's for the night porter,

Damian. He spends his days sleeping and writing books.'

'You said you have an apartment here?' Ben asked.

'Damian and I have basement studio apartments,' Ted confirmed.

'There's an underground garage?'

'Below our studio apartments, for the family's vehicles and Mr Barnes's business vehicles.'

'Why does a restaurant owner need vehicles?' Ben frowned.

'He has a central kitchen that bakes cakes and desserts. They're frozen and shipped out to his own and other restaurants, and to gourmet food shops.'

'Have you noticed anything out of the ordinary on the CCTV today?' Amy moved alongside Ben.

'No, but I wasn't here all morning. I had to fix a leak under the sink in the studio.'

'What time was that?' Ben reached for his notebook and pen.

'After Mrs Barnes left, because I

was at my desk when she walked out.'

'Time?' Amy prompted.

'I went up after the post had been delivered at half past eleven and came down about quarter past twelve.'

'That's when you found the box on the desk?'

'Yes.'

'You didn't see who left it there?'

'I knew it had to be someone in the building. I locked the doors when I went up to the artists' studio, as I always do whenever I leave the desk.'

'What if anyone wants to come in?' Amy looked up from her notebook.

'The residents have their own key codes. Visitors can press the intercom.'

'You would have answered them?'

Ted produced a small box from under the desk. 'This is a receiver for the transmitter in the intercom. I always take it with me whenever I leave the foyer.

'If an officer comes looking for us, Mr Levett, we'll be interviewing Michael Barnes and Anni Jones,' Amy informed him.

'The sergeant wouldn't allow them into their studio or apartment. They're in the conference suite.'

'Are Michael Barnes and Anni Jones the only two residents in there?' Amy checked.

Before Ted could answer, a piercing scream came from the conference centre.

The door crashed back on its hinges.

'You'll have to kill me first.' A young woman rushed out, pursued by a young man and a constable.

CHAPTER THIRTEEN

The constable and young man managed to subdue the woman. They escorted her back into the conference suite. Amy and Ben followed.

'Please, Miss Jones, calm yourself.' The constable blocked the doorway.

'You're threatening to destroy five years of my work and you're asking me to keep calm . . .'

'Are you senior officers?' The man demanded.

'Inspector Amy Stuart and Sergeant Ben Miller,' Amy introduced herself and Ben.

'Your constables are threatening to smash my girlfriend's sculptures. They're preventing us from entering our studio. We have to deliver artwork to an exhibition. If we don't, it could cost us our reputations, as well as a great deal of money,' he raged.

'You are Mr Michael Barnes and Miss Anni Jones?'

'We are,' Michael retorted. 'Just what the hell is going on?' Michael was a younger version of his brother—slimmer, with sharper features. There was a suspicious expression in his eyes. Annoyance at being kept from his apartment and studio? Or something more sinister? Amy wondered.

'Please don't damage my sculptures,' Anni begged. 'I promised to deliver them to a Knightsbridge gallery today. If I don't, they could cancel my exhibition.'

'Have you any idea how competitive the art world is? Or how much work Anni has put in—'

Amy interrupted Michael. 'Have you seen your sister-in-law, or Mr Bruno Gambrini, or Mr Adrian Wills today?'

'No,' Michael snarled.

'You're sure?' Amy pressed.

'Of course I'm sure.' Michael raised his voice. 'We've only seen Jack today . . .'

'When?'

'He gave us a hand to move one of our sculptures into the lift first thing . . .'

'What time was "first thing"?'

Michael looked to Anni. 'Eight, eight thirty?'

'About then,' she agreed.

'Then what did you do?' Amy asked.

'We loaded our van . . .'

'Is it kept in the garage here?' Ben looked up from his notebook.

'Yes.'

'Registration number?'

Michael rattled it off.

'Big van?'

'A transit. We need it to transport Anni's sculptures. They're life size.'

'How long did it take you to load up?' Amy continued the interview.

'An hour. We took four sculptures from the studio. That's as many as the van can take.'

'You drove away from the building, when?' Ben poised his pen over his notepad.

'Nine thirty,' Anni answered.

'You're very sure,' Amy

commented.

'I checked my watch as we left. I remember telling Michael it was a good time to set off because we were missing the rush hour.'

'You drove straight to the gallery?' Amy checked.

'Straight there,' Michael echoed. 'Then we unloaded Anni's sculptures. She stayed to arrange them.'

'You didn't stay?' Ben looked up.

'The exhibition is Anni's, not mine. I drove to Hyde Park and walked our dog.' He pointed to a Pekinese lying under a chair.

'Where exactly did you go in the park?'

Michael lost his temper. 'What's this? You're not allowed to walk a dog in the park without telling the police . . . ?'

In contrast to Michael, Amy kept cool. 'What time did you arrive at the gallery?'

'Ten o'clock.' It was Anni, not

Michael, who spoke.

'Did you see anyone there?'

'Julie Harris, the owner, and her employees, George and Yolanda.' Again it was Anni who answered.

'What time did you leave?'

'Michael left about half past ten . . .'

'I've had enough.' Michael declared. 'I'll not say another word until you tell me what this is about.'

'If you can't produce any witnesses as to your whereabouts this morning, would you like to continue this discussion at the police station?' Ben enquired.

'We arrived at the gallery at ten o'clock,' Anni answered for Michael. 'We had to wait ten minutes for a spot in the loading bay. Julie and her staff helped us unload. It took about half an hour. Afterwards, Michael left for the park. He returned at half past twelve. We drove back via Kensington Gardens. We found a parking space, bought sandwiches and orange juice, had a picnic lunch, stayed about half an hour, then returned here.'

'Kensington Gardens is out of your way, isn't it?' Ben asked.

'Anni was envious of my walk in the park. She wanted to see something green. Is that a crime?' Michael was still fuming.

'Did you meet anyone you knew in the park or the gardens?' Amy checked.

'No.'

'Were there many people about?'

'Hyde Park on a dry Valentine's Day morning. Hundreds,' Michael glared at Ben. 'And the same goes for the gardens.'

Amy's mobile rang. She left the room, closed the door behind her and walked to the corner of the foyer furthest from the porter's desk. 'Amy Stuart.'

Patrick answered in his Irish lilt. 'We've had the DNA results on the heart.'

81

CHAPTER FOURTEEN

'And . . . ?' It irritated Amy, having to ask.

'It's Zee Barnes.'

'Does Jack Barnes know?'

'Barbara Davies is on her way to him with Irene Conway, the family liaison officer.' Patrick ended the call. Amy switched off her mobile and looked through the glass panel. Michael was still shouting at Ben.

*   *   *

Ted's voice was low, apologetic. 'I'm sorry, Miss Leila. The police are searching the building. No one's allowed into their apartments.'

Amy turned to see the porter talking to a well-groomed woman in her forties. She could have posed for a fashion magazine aimed at the middle-aged.

'The police?' Leila repeated. 'What on earth are the police doing in the building?'

Amy went to the desk. 'I'll speak to Miss Barnes, Ted.'

Leila glared at Amy. 'And you are?'

'Inspector Amy Stuart. If you'll join me in the conference suite, I'll explain what's happening.'

'Join you?' Leila repeated in disgust. 'This is not your building, Inspector Stuart. You've no authority to issue invitations. I wish to go to my apartment. Now.'

'I need to speak to you first, Miss Barnes.' Amy opened the door of the conference suite. Ben was still trying to calm Michael. 'Miss Barnes, if you'd sit down please.'

'I don't want to sit—'

'For pity's sake, Leila, don't be your usual difficult self. Not with these people, or they'll keep us here for ever.' Michael snapped at his sister.

'No one's told me what's going on . . .'

'Please sit down, Miss Barnes.' Amy glanced at Ben.

Leila sat three chairs away from her brother and his girlfriend.

Amy looked at Ben again to make sure he was watching the faces of Leila, Michael and Ann. 'I regret to inform you that your sister-in-law, Zee Barnes, and the chef Bruno Gambrini have been murdered.'

'There must be some mistake . . .'

'I assure you there's no mistake, Miss Barnes.'

Anni slumped back in her chair. 'Zee—and Bruno . . .' She began to cry: large, soft, silent tears.

'Where's Jack?' Michael asked.

'In his office.'

'Is anyone with him?' Leila asked. 'He shouldn't be alone . . .'

'He's not alone,' Amy assured her.

'I suppose that secretary of his—'

'For heaven's sake, Leila, shut up.' Michael looked at Amy. 'How was

Zee killed? Did the same person kill her and Bruno . . . ?'

'I'm not at liberty to divulge any more information, Mr Barnes.'

'Have you caught whoever's responsible?'

'We need to interview everyone who lives in the building. Miss Barnes, could I speak to you first?' Amy opened an inner door, which led on to a corridor.

'There are four offices and four en-suite bedrooms in there,' Michael explained. 'If you want somewhere private, there's an office ahead of you.'

'Thank you.' Amy opened the door that Michael indicated. 'Miss Barnes?'

Leila left her chair reluctantly.

A constable tapped Amy on the shoulder. 'Liam Ansell has reviewed the CCTV images, ma'am. There's something he thinks you should see right away.'

CHAPTER FIFTEEN

Amy and Ben left Michael, Leila and Anni with the constable and entered the conference room, which had been transformed into an incident room.

Half a dozen officers were talking on phones. Others were moving desks, fixing photographs to Perspex screens and inputting information on computers. Sergeant Reece and Liam Ansell were at a desk in a corner. A bank of screens had been installed above it. Liam smiled when he saw Amy. He and Amy had once been close. Although he hadn't wanted their relationship to end, they'd managed to split amicably enough to remain friends.

'I've collated the last images of Zee Barnes, ma'am. Before you see them, there's something else you should look at.' Liam hit a series of buttons. Images of the corridors of Barnes Building filled the screen.

Amy noted the time in the corner of the screens. 'Twelve twenty-three. Today?'

'Yes, ma'am. This is the corridor outside Bruno Gambrini's apartment. There it is. It's present for less than two seconds. I'll freeze it.'

'A figure in chefs' whites and hat exiting Bruno Gambrini's door.' Ben said. 'At twelve twenty-three, when Adrian Wills didn't enter the building until twelve fifty.'

'Has that time been verified?' Amy asked.

'By the restaurant Adrian works in, the taxi driver who drove him here, and the porter,' Sergeant Reece confirmed.

'Look up, damn it,' Ben ordered.

'Unfortunately, whoever it is doesn't show their face,' Liam answered.

'Can you make that image clearer?' Ben asked.

'That's as clear as it can get, sir.'

Amy studied the blurred figure. 'Given the position of the light switch, I'd say five feet nine inches.'

'Agreed. Medium build, not a shred of hair to be seen beneath that hat. And, as we only have a back view of someone in baggy clothing, holding what looks like a black sack, they could be male or female,' Ben added.

'More sightings?' Amy looked at Liam.

'Not of our mystery figure in chefs' whites, but this was recorded between ten past two and ten past three this morning.'

'The corridors are empty,' Ben said irritably.

'Look closer. Here and here.' Liam moved the mouse arrow over the edges of the screen. 'The light dims. Something or someone has blocked the lamps in the corridor.'

Amy peered closer. 'Shadows?'

'Someone is moving out of camera

range,' Liam declared.

'We checked security,' Sergeant Reece said. 'The outside doors are locked day and night. The only way in is with a resident who has a key code or through the porter.'

'A resident would know the location of the cameras,' Amy said.

'See, movement again here.' Liam indicated an area where a shadow flickered.

'Could be someone familiar with the location of the cameras,' Ben mused. 'Possibly the someone in chefs' whites who was too rattled after killing Bruno to be careful?'

'It's a theory,' Amy acknowledged. 'Is there only one key code for all the apartments?'

'No. I checked with the porter,' Sergeant Reece informed her. 'Each resident has their own code to the front door and a different code for their apartment.'

'And if they tried to enter another apartment?' Ben asked.

'An alarm would trigger and freeze the lock.'

'Is there a master code that overrides the individual codes?' Ben stared at the screen.

'Yes, but only the porters and Jack Barnes have it.'

'Is there a record of when it's used as opposed to the individual codes?'

'Yes, ma'am, and the locks are being checked by a technician. But she warned us not to expect results for a couple of hours.'

'So, we've someone creeping around the building between ten past two and five past three in the morning. But all we can see are shadows.'

'It happened again this morning, ma'am,' Liam added.

'What time and where in the building?'

'The first shadow appears at seven minutes past eleven on the fourth floor.'

Amy referred to her notebook.

'The artists' studio floor?'

Liam called up the screen. 'Yes. The shadow crosses the light above the fire exit, then disappears.'

'Can you see it in any other corridors?' Amy asked.

'There's a flicker four minutes later on the camera above the door to the underground garage.'

Amy looked at Sergeant Reece. 'Wouldn't you need a key code to get out of the building as well as into it?'

'Yes, ma'am.'

'Get the codes used on that lock checked as a priority.'

The sergeant signalled to a constable.

'Do you want to see the last images we have of Mrs Barnes, ma'am?' Liam looked enquiringly at Amy.

'Please.' Amy found it harrowing to view CCTV images of any victim going about their daily life before a crime, but murders were the worst. She was dreading seeing a live Zee

Barnes walking, smiling; no longer a victim but a living breathing person.

'We're missing something,' Ben said.

'What?' Amy looked at him.

'Anyone coming in here has to get past the porter, right?'

'Right,' Sergeant Reece confirmed.

'The porter has given us a timeline accounting for every resident's movements this morning, but he admits to being away from his desk from roughly eleven thirty to twelve fifteen.'

'Agreed,' Amy answered.

'Everyone is accounted for except—this mystery figure in chefs' whites, who is seen leaving Bruno's apartment, carrying a black sack, approximately half an hour before Bruno Gambrini was found murdered.'

'Your point is?' Amy pressed.

'Bruno's murder was messy. If this someone is Bruno's murderer, they could have knifed Bruno, changed into his chefs' whites and carried their own bloodstained clothing away in the sack. In which case, where is it?'

'Sergeant Reece, get the porter,' Amy ordered.

CHAPTER SIXTEEN

Amy and Ben left the search of the rubbish chutes and bins to Sergeant Reece. They returned to the office where they'd left Leila Barnes.

'How was Zee murdered?' Leila asked when they entered.

'We're not at liberty to divulge that, Miss Barnes,' Amy answered.

'I'm her sister-in-law,' Leila protested.

'We'll get through this interview more quickly if you co-operate, Miss Barnes,' Amy warned. 'Where were you this morning?'

'You can't regard me as a

suspect . . .'

'Please, Miss Barnes, answer our questions.' Ben flashed an insincere smile.

'I left the building at eight thirty to take Mamie, that's my younger sister, to school. I returned at nine o'clock. I wrote some letters on my return and didn't go out again until about a quarter to one when I left for a charity committee meeting.'

'Letters? You worked on a computer?' Amy questioned.

'Some of the time. I also drafted notes by hand for the meeting.'

'Did you see or speak to anyone when you were in your apartment?

'Obviously I didn't see anyone. I made several telephone calls.'

'Time of the calls?'

'I can't remember,' Leila snapped angrily.

Amy watched Ben make a note to check Leila's calls and computer log. 'The name of the charity and place you met?'

'St Anna's Hospice. We use the conference room in the offices.'

'Time?'

'One o'clock. Several committee members work, so we arrange our meetings at lunchtime.'

Amy looked at the timeline Ted had given her. 'Zee left her apartment just after eleven o'clock. She placed cards and roses outside your door.'

'I saw them when I left.'

'Zee didn't knock on your door?'

'If she did, I didn't hear her, but I could have been on the telephone or in the bathroom.'

'Would you describe your relationship with Zee as close?'

'She's more than twenty years younger than me. We have different interests.'

'How would you describe your sister-in-law?' Amy pressed.

'In a word: devious. She wormed her way into Jack's affections when he was grieving for his first wife.'

'Your brother's first wife died?' Amy sat forward.

'In a fire in a castle that Jack was renovating in Wales. Jack was devastated. Jodie—his first wife—was pregnant at the time. It was heartbreaking. Michael and I thought that was why Zee got herself pregnant so soon after meeting Jack. She knew he'd marry her if there was a child on the way. I only wish I could have been as sure as Jack that the child was his.'

'What made you think Jack wasn't the father?' Ben asked.

'Jack never said a word—to me or Michael—about planning to have a child with Zee. But Jack was besotted. He wouldn't listen to reason once Zee announced her pregnancy. It worried Michael and me.'

'Why?' Amy probed.

'Zee was fifteen years younger than Jack. Pretty enough, in a common way, but she'd barely been educated. She was neither a social nor an intellectual match for Jack.'

'What caused the fire that killed Jodie?' Ben was interested.

'Faulty electrical wiring. The electrician was fined for negligence. Not enough, in my opinion.'

'You said Jack was devastated,' Amy reminded her.

'I thought he'd have a breakdown.'

'But he made a recovery?' Amy prompted.

'Once he started dating Zee, four months after Jodie's death. He married her a week after she told him she was pregnant.'

'You thought that was too quick?' Ben suggested.

'Yes, but Jack's always been a womaniser. For all his insistence he loved Jodie, he couldn't stop playing around with other women.'

'Your brother's first marriage wasn't happy?' Amy asked.

'In my opinion, that was only because each ignored what the other was doing. As for Zee . . . well,' Leila pursed her lips. 'It's not for me to speak ill of the dead.'

'In what way?' Ben enquired.

'Ted Levett,' Leila spat out his name. 'I couldn't believe it when Zee brought him here. Old school friend indeed—'

'Yet Jack employed him,' Ben interrupted.

'Because Zee asked him to and he couldn't refuse her anything. It was obvious what Zee and Ted were up to,' Leila declared. 'I saw them giggling and touching one another at all hours of the day and night. Every time they saw me watching, they'd stop and pretend Zee was just passing through the foyer.'

'Did Jack say anything to you about Zee's relationship with Ted?' Amy set her notebook on the desk.

'No. I think he ignored it because in his eyes Zee could do no wrong.'

'Are you saying he was faithful to Zee but not to Jodie?' Amy checked.

'Jack was besotted with Zee but I doubt he was faithful to her. It's not in his nature. He doesn't only have an office above his restaurant. There's an apartment with a hot tub and luxury bedroom and bathroom. Possibly he takes his women there.'

'You've seen it?' Ben was surprised.

'Mamie and I stayed there for a few nights when the heating failed in our apartment last winter. But, as I said, Jack's always been the same. He'll chase after any woman who flashes a smile and a thigh. I think that's why he encouraged Jodie to buy a place she could retreat to in Wales when he was working—or so he claimed.'

'Why Wales?' Amy was curious.

'Jodie had family there. Jack thought it would be a good idea for her to have her own place close to her mother.'

'Was Jodie happy about it?' Ben queried.

'She didn't complain, but Jodie was a saint compared to Zee. Pretty, educated, she'd lectured in ancient history before marrying Jack. Zee was a waitress; a nobody when she flung herself at Jack.'

'Your brother must have thought something of Zee to marry her,' Ben commented.

'As I said, he married her only after she told him she was pregnant. He showered her with presents. Gave her a credit card and paid the bills every month. Money was no object after Zee moved in with Jack.'

'Did Jack complain about Zee's spending?'

'I keep telling you, Inspector, he was blind to her faults, but I saw through her. She tried to take over my charity work. Asked if she could help, then claimed credit for my efforts. Well, I wasn't having that. That's why I wouldn't answer the door to her this morning . . .' Leila faltered.

'You knew Zee knocked on your door this morning, yet you didn't answer it?' Amy recalled the roses and cards that Zee had delivered to everyone.

'I knew it was Zee. Anyone coming in from outside would have been announced on the intercom by the doorman. I looked through the spyhole, saw her standing there and walked away. I have better things to do with my time than waste it on Zee.'

Amy looked up at a knock on the door. 'Come in.'

'Sergeant Reece is asking if you can come upstairs immediately, ma'am. It's urgent.'

CHAPTER SEVENTEEN

Amy and Ben heard the shouting before the lift doors opened on to the studio floor.

'Damn, I forgot about the sculptures.' Amy ran into the studio. Sergeant Reece was speaking slowly, calmly—in contrast to Anni Jones, who was hysterical.

'No, you can't break open that sculpture. You'll kill it. I'll not allow it. It took me months . . .'

'Don't you dare touch it.' Michael Barnes grabbed a constable, who was moving towards one of the sculptures that lined the studio walls.

'Everyone stop!' Amy shouted at the constables who were searching the room.

'We're being careful, ma'am,' Sergeant Reece reassured Amy.

'Those sculptures are a nightmare.' Ben stared at the life-sized pieces.

Amy gazed at the bronze and marble sculptures. 'The bronzes have been cast for some time.' She wrapped her fingers in a tissue and tapped the marble sculptures that depicted the same man and woman in a series of classical poses. 'And these are solid. They're also excellent.'

'Now you're an art critic?' Michael mocked.

'No, but I studied fine art at college. You want to move these?'

'Some of them,' Anni confirmed.

'The bronze and marble sculptures can be moved, Sergeant Reece,' Amy said.

'And these? Your savages want to cut them open.' Michael indicated a row of colourful papier-mâché fairytale figures. They ranged from witches, goblins and princesses to dwarves and giants. Like the bronzes and marble, all were life size.

'My children's range,' Anni explained.

'You sell them?' Ben was amazed.

'To toy shops, children's theatres, and to people who buy them for their children's rooms.'

Ben tapped a witch. It echoed hollowly.

'You damage it, you pay. They fetch over four thousand pounds—each,' Michael warned.

'Want to cut them open?' Ben asked Amy.

'What on earth for?' Michael questioned angrily.

'We haven't found Zee's body.' Amy watched Michael and Anni as she spoke.

'If you haven't found her body, how do you know she's dead?' Michael demanded.

'I'm not at—'

'Liberty to divulge,' Michael finished for her.

Amy turned to Anni. 'There are joins down the side.'

'They're made in pieces and welded together with resin. Please don't damage them. As Michael said, I've put two years' work into this exhibition. The gallery owner picked out the pieces she wanted. I can't let her down by delivering an incomplete list.'

Amy thought for a moment. 'Can you see if we can get the dogs at short notice?'

'Cadaver or blood?' Ben asked.

'Both. Meanwhile, you can take out the marble and bronze sculptures,' she advised Michael and Anni, 'but none of these papier mâché figures.'

'I can't wait for dogs. They have to be at the gallery tonight. I promised,' Anni pleaded.

'Then we cut them,' Amy declared. 'Your choice? What's it to be?'

'Will just one suit you?' Michael picked up a Stanley knife and inserted a blade.

'Michael . . .' Anni began.

'If you want to get these to the exhibition, Anni, you're going to have to sacrifice one. Once these idiots see the weights inside them, they'll let the rest through.' He looked at Amy. 'Pick one, but only one.'

CHAPTER EIGHTEEN

Amy looked along the row. She chose a witch, simply because there were two similar sculptures.

Anni turned her face to the wall. 'I can't look.'

Michael sliced down the sides of the figure. He finished by lying it flat on its back and cutting round its head and feet before pulling the two halves apart. 'Satisfied?' he demanded of Amy.

Amy turned to the sergeant. 'Compare the weight of every papier-mâché sculpture removed from this studio with that one. If any appear unusually heavy, leave it here.'

'Yes, ma'am.'

*   *   *

Amy and Ben returned to the incident room. Ben pulled up a

couple of chairs and set them in front of Liam's desk. Exhausted, Amy sat between the men.

'This is the first sighting of Zee Barnes, ma'am.' Liam slowed the tape.

Amy watched the door of the penthouse open. Zee emerged. A shadowy figure was in the doorway behind her. 'Her cleaner?'

'Sara Hilger,' Ben noted the time in the corner of the screen. 'Eleven oh-one a.m.'

The door closed. Zee walked to the lift and pressed the button. As Amy had feared, she found the images disturbing. She wanted to wind the clock back. To stand in front of Zee and demand that she return to her apartment—and safety.

'Zee entering the lift, riding down one floor,' Liam commented.

The image of Zee in the lift wasn't as clear as the one in the hall. The film was grainy. Zee was wearing a light-coloured suit. Her blonde hair appeared paler than her clothes, her handbag and shoes darker.

'Leaving the lift on the floor below her apartment,' Liam continued.

'Eleven oh-four.' Ben noted.

'Knocking on the door, moving to the stairs, reappearing outside the artists' studio. Leaving flowers and cards. Disappearing back to the stairs. Reappearing on the floor below the artists' studio.'

'Leila and Mamie's apartment,' Ben commented.

'Knocking on the door. Waiting for a reply. One minute,' Liam observed.

'That's a long time; you'd think she'd realise no one was in.'

'The apartments are vast,' Amy reminded Ben. 'You could fit ten of mine into one of them. If someone was on the balcony, it could take them a minute to answer the door.' Amy watched Zee take cards and rosebuds from her oversized handbag. She laid them in front of the door before walking through the fire doors to the stairs and vanishing. 'There are no cameras on the stairs?' Amy checked.

'Only the exits to the street and yard,' Liam confirmed.

Zee was next seen outside Bruno Gambrini's apartment, where she again left flowers and cards.

'She didn't knock,' Ben murmured.

'Probably assumed the chefs had left for work,' Amy suggested.

Zee left the lift in the foyer at 11.10. She approached the porter's desk and spoke to Ted.

Amy studied Zee, looking for signs in her body language that might indicate she was having an affair with the porter. 'I wish I could hear what they're saying.'

'I wish I could see the expressions on their faces,' Ben added.

'They seem friendly but not over-friendly,' Liam interposed. 'She's there for thirteen minutes. I'll bring up the outside CCTV images on the screen to the right.'

The officers followed Zee's progress. She left Ted and the foyer through the automatic doors. She hesitated in front of the building for forty-two seconds, lifted her arm, looked at her watch and turned right.

'These are the last sightings,' Liam warned. 'When she leaves the area covered by the building's CCTV, she appears on the one fixed in front of the florist's a block away.'

'You fetched that tape this morning?' Amy asked.

'I put in a request for all the CCTV images covering this street between eleven o'clock and one o'clock, which was when I arrived.'

'Efficient.'

'I try, ma'am,' Liam responded dryly.

'Sorry,' Amy apologised. 'I didn't mean to patronise.'

'Zee walking past the florist's.' Liam looked back at the screen.

'Eleven twenty-three.' Ben noted the time.

'She stops, looks at the flowers. Turns. Something's attracted her attention,' Ben remarked.

'She looks over her shoulder, steps back alongside the van, and that's it. She disappears.' Liam froze the frames before replaying them.

'Go back one,' Amy ordered. 'That van in front of the florist.'

'She could have got into it,' Ben agreed, 'but she could also have entered the shop, or climbed into the Fiat parked in front of the van, or the BMW behind it.'

'Has anyone visited the florist?' Amy asked Sergeant Reece.

'Sergeant Reece sent constables to check out the premises two hundred yards either side of this building. Only the florist remembered seeing Zee. When he was out at the front arranging flowers, he noticed a lady from Barnes Building stopping to look at the display.'

'The van?' Ben prompted. 'The BMW and Fiat? Have they been

traced?'

A constable approached the desk. 'The results have come in on the Fiat, van and BMW, Sergeant.'

Sergeant Reece left his chair.

CHAPTER NINETEEN

'How's that for efficiency, Inspector Miller?' Liam took the paper that the constable handed him. 'The Fiat belongs to the florist. The BMW is owned by a local resident. He's an editor and returned to pick up a manuscript he'd forgotten to take to work.'

'The van?' Amy questioned.

Liam fast-tracked the images until they showed the transit driving away. 'It was parked too close to the BMW and Fiat for the number to register on CCTV. Once it pulled out into the traffic, it was out of range of the street cameras. It left the kerb at eleven thirty-seven a.m. and was caught on a speed camera at the end of the road at eleven forty a.m. See the number plate.'

Amy frowned. 'It looks blank.'

'It's been painted with photo-blocker paint.'

'What's photo-blocker paint?' Ben asked.

'It's invisible when painted on. But when the plate passes a speed camera the paint produces a high-powered gloss that reflects light back to the camera. It overexposes the image, which makes the plate unreadable.'

'This paint is legal?' Ben asked.

'It's legal. You've never worked in the traffic division, sir,' Liam commented.

'Any distinguishing marks on the van?' Amy asked Liam.

'It's a white transit, like a few thousand others in London. We can't be sure that the paint is a ruse. Hundreds if not thousands of vehicles have photo-blocker paint on their plates. The van might not be connected to Zee Barnes's disappearance at all.'

*   *   *

Sergeant Reece returned to the incident room. He, Ben and Amy retreated to a smaller office. Amy closed the door.

'Nothing in the artists' studio, ma'am. I sent a constable to the gallery with Anni Jones and Michael Barnes,' Sergeant Reece reported. 'And no clothing—bloodstained or otherwise—in the skips or rubbish chutes. I've sent for a dog handler. Forensic are working on stains on the floor of the boiler house. There's an incinerator there.'

'Good work, and you can call me Amy when we're in senior officer-conference, Sergeant. I remember playing football with you and Dad when I was small.'

114

'I never thought that one day you'd be my boss. The name's David.'

'I remember—David. First, let me thank you and your team for all the work you've done in such a short time.' She opened a file. 'Let's start with the timeline. Ben, you've kept a record.'

Ben referred to his notebook. 'Shadows moving in the corridors, picked up on CCTV between two fifteen and three oh-five a.m. First noticed on the studio floor.'

'The only floor no one lives on,' David Reece commented.

'Then seen on the floor the chefs live on at two nineteen . . .'

'Could have been the murderer picking up the knives?' David interrupted.

'We can't be sure the knives found in the sink and the one that killed Bruno Gambrini belonged to the chefs.'

'They match other knives in the apartment,' David said.

'I'd like to interview Adrian Wills and get the forensic results on the knives before coming to any conclusions.'

Ben continued. 'A shadow appears at the basement garage door at two twenty-five a.m.'

'Has the garage been searched?' Amy asked.

'Only around the vehicles.'

'Organise a search of every vehicle, with the dogs if you can get them. Tell the officers to break into the vans if necessary.'

David reached for his mobile.

Ben resumed when David had given the order. 'There was a twenty-minute lull before shadows were seen in the reverse order, ending on the studio floor at three oh-one. At eleven ten this morning, shadows appeared again on the studio floor.'

'When Zee Barnes was entering the foyer,' Amy commented.

'There was another on the basement garage floor at eleven

fifteen a.m.,' Ben murmured.

'Is there a camera logging the vans in and out?' Amy asked.

'Yes,' David answered. 'Attached to the barrier. It snaps number plates as the vehicles enter and exit.'

'Something else that needs checking, David. Phone the order through.'

David did as Amy asked.

'So we have a someone—'

Ben interrupted. 'Could be more than one person.'

'A person or people,' Amy conceded, 'creeping around Barnes Building in the early hours, and again the following morning. We have Zee Barnes exiting her apartment just after eleven. Leaving flowers and Valentine cards . . .'

'For everyone in the building, including her sister-in-law who didn't answer the door.' Ben followed the timeline in his notes.

'Zee Barnes spoke to Ted Levett for thirteen minutes, stepped outside the building just before eleven twenty-three, then turned right and vanished in daylight in front of a florist's.'

'If she entered a vehicle and was driven away, her body could be miles away,' David declared.

'I doubt it,' Ben said. 'It would take time to remove her heart. It was on the porter's desk at twelve fifteen. I'd say our killer is a quick worker who has access to a local safe place.'

'Not in Barnes Building—we've searched everywhere,' David insisted.

'Zee Barnes was kidnapped, murdered, had her heart removed and parcelled up in fifty-two minutes,' Ben declared. 'That suggests the killer or killers knew Zee, and also knew Barnes Building—and the residents' movements.'

'Ted saw the parcel at twelve fifteen but it could have been on the desk for longer. It was left on the one spot on the porter's desk that is out of CCTV range,' David observed.

'The courier picked up the parcel at twelve twenty. Jack Barnes received it ten minutes later.' Amy stared thoughtfully at the last stills of Zee that Liam had printed.

'Whoever killed Zee Barnes had access to this building,' David stated. 'No stranger could have left the heart without alerting a porter. We've interviewed both. They insist no one called between Zee's departure and the arrival of the courier Ted summoned.'

'Let's eliminate the residents with solid alibis,' Ben suggested. 'To start at the top of the building: Jack Barnes arrived at his office before Zee left the apartment. He remained there with his staff until the heart was delivered. The cleaner, Sara, left the building half an hour after Zee disappeared.'

'Both are in the clear, but we should interview the cleaner for background information on Zee.' Amy marked Sara's name on her own list. 'Michael Barnes and Anni Jones?'

'Anni Jones was at the gallery until twelve thirty. We're checking CCTV around the Hyde Park area for a sighting of Michael Barnes. Without it, he has no alibi.' David scribbled a question mark next to Michael's name. 'But I can't see what motive he'd have to kill his sister-in-law.'

'Leave the motive for the moment,' Amy ordered.

'Leila and Mamie Barnes,' Ben continued. 'Mamie's at school, so her movements should be easy enough to check. Leila was in all morning and didn't leave the building until twenty to one. Count them out?'

'Not Leila. Not until we've checked her computer and phone records,' Amy said decisively.

'Adrian Wills was at a market at six thirty a.m. He arrived at the restaurant at eight o'clock and left at twelve thirty-five. So he could have killed Bruno but not Zee,' David said. 'I sent a constable to the restaurant. According to the staff, Adrian was furious with Bruno for not turning up for work. At ten o'clock, Jack Barnes sent a messenger round to check Bruno was all right, but Bruno didn't open the door to him. At ten thirty Jack sent a doctor who did gain admittance, examined Bruno and diagnosed a hangover.'

'Adrian would have had to kill Bruno quickly, and there's the sighting of the mystery figure in chefs' whites,' Amy said thoughtfully. 'But I agree, whether Adrian killed Bruno or not, he couldn't have killed Zee.'

'The porters know the building, the residents and their movements. Both were alone for most of the morning.'

Ben added Ted Levett and Damian Clark's names to his list.

'That makes three people who had the opportunity to kill Zee and Bruno, and one who could have killed Bruno.'

Amy's phone rang the same time as David's. Amy's conversation was short. She ended the call and said, 'The blood on the knives found in the sink in Bruno Gambrini's apartment is confirmed as belonging to Zee Barnes.'

'The number plate on one of the vans in the basement garage has been painted with photo-blocker paint. I told them to wait for us before opening it.' David left his chair.

CHAPTER TWENTY

Amy looked around the under-ground garage. 'It's larger than I expected.'

'It extends under the yard at the

back as well as the building.' David had studied the architect's plans.

'There have to be fifty vans here, as well as the cars.' Ben eyed the Rolls-Royce, Mercedes, Alfa Romeos and BMWs lined up in front of the door that connected with Barnes Building.

'Sixty-two vans and eighteen cars.' David consulted the list a junior officer had drawn up. 'The Rolls and three other cars belong to Jack Barnes. Zee drove the gold BMW. The rest belong to the other residents. Michael Barnes also owns a van.'

'And the twelve-year-old Astra?' Ben asked. The battered, rust-spotted car was parked some distance from the Barnes's cars.

'Belongs to the night porter, Damian. Ted Levett doesn't have a car.' David waved to an officer. 'The van with the plates painted with photo-blocker is over there, ma'am.'

'The darkest corner,' Amy

observed. The wall lights were low illumination and set more than five metres apart.

They headed for the van, which was parked in the furthest corner from the street exit. Spotlights had been set up around it. The bodywork glistened with fingerprint powder. Two officers—suited, booted with gloves and hats—were waiting, skeleton keys in hand.

'Prints?' Amy asked.

'Only smudges, ma'am.' The officer handed out sheets of paper. 'Information on the van.'

'It was reported stolen?' Ben said.

'Over a week ago.'

'But it was owned by Jack Barnes?' Ben checked.

'His company, sir.'

'Anyone notice it here before today?' Amy moved close to a spotlight and scanned the sheet.

'No one we've spoken to, ma'am.'

Amy went to the box of protective clothing and handed one suit to Ben and another to David. When they'd finished covering their clothes, she nodded to the officer holding the keys.

'The cab first, ma'am?'

'Yes.'

The officer opened the door and shone a torch inside. 'Street maps of London.' He pushed the bundle aside with his gloved hand. 'Plug in satnav, newspaper. Brown paper bag . . .'

'Careful,' David warned.

'It contains a half-eaten sausage roll covered in mould, sir.'

'Anything on the floor?' Amy asked.

'Footprints, ma'am.'

'Leave them for now, we'll check the back. Dust the entire cab for prints—finger, foot and swab for DNA.'

'Yes, ma'am.' The officer slammed the door and walked to the side door. He opened it and reeled back into Ben.

Ben picked up the torch the officer had dropped. He shone it into the van.

Amy had been a police officer for four years. She thought she'd seen all the horrors of life. But she'd never been faced with anything like the interior of that van.

*   *   *

'It's a slaughterhouse.'

Amy heard Ben but was too stunned to reply.

David Reece walked a few steps and vomited. He slumped against the wall. Tears were running down his cheeks. 'Did you see her face?' he whispered hoarsely. 'Her eyes. I've never seen such terror in a corpse's eyes.'

*   *   *

The barrier lifted at the entrance to the car park. The constable manning it stepped in front of the incoming car.

Ben whispered to Amy. 'Jack Barnes has arrived.'

Amy assumed command. 'Sergeant Reece, close the van. Call the pathologist and forensic teams and order them here.'

'What about formally identifying the body?' David Reece was pale, still trembling.

'The DNA of the heart delivered to Jack Barnes has been identified. The corpse in that van is female, dressed in a similar outfit to the one Zee Barnes was wearing on CCTV. The corpse's chest is open, the heart missing. All the evidence points to the body being Zee Barnes, Sergeant Reece.' Amy knew she was being unfair to David but, after seeing what was left of Zee Barnes, she was struggling to maintain her self-control.

Jack got out of the car, accompanied by his secretary, Alice, and by the police family liaison officer, Irene Conway. His face was drained of colour. His shoulders stooped. He had aged twenty years in the few hours since Amy and Ben had seen him at midday.

'Inspector Stuart?'

'You have your orders,' Ben barked at the assembled officers. They all left, including David Reece.

Amy waited until the officers were out of earshot. 'We've found your wife's body, Mr Barnes. I'm sorry . . .'

'You told me you'd keep me informed of developments,' he reproached her.

'We only discovered her a few minutes ago.'

'Where?' Jack's voice was harsh.

'In this van. It's one of yours, reported stolen a week ago.'

Jack reached for the door handle. Ben caught his hand before he touched it. 'The crime scene has to be preserved for the forensic teams, sir.'

'You opened the van?' Jack challenged.

'We're wearing protective clothing and we didn't step inside,' Amy informed him.

'Have you got a suit I can wear?'

'Please, Mr Barnes, believe me, you don't want to see inside that van,' Amy pleaded.

'I have a right to see my wife.' He glared at her.

Amy realised that Jack Barnes was a powerful man who was used to getting his own way. She was sure that if she offered a platitude like 'remembering his wife the way she'd been when he'd said goodbye to her that morning', he would brush it aside, but she persisted. 'The pathologist will have to do a post mortem. The scene can't be disturbed . . .'

'I have no intention of disturbing the crime scene. I only want to look at my wife.' He continued to stare at her.

After a full minute of strained tension, during which Jack didn't blink, Ben handed Jack Barnes a suit, hat, gloves, overshoes and a mask before donning a mask himself. He gave one to Amy.

Amy tried one last warning. 'Experienced officers have been affected by the sight of your wife's corpse, Mr Barnes. Are you sure you want me to open this door?'

'Get on with it.'

CHAPTER TWENTY-ONE

Alice and Irene stepped back behind Jack.

Amy tugged the handle and slid the door open.

Jack stared, wide-eyed above the white paper mask.

'Catch him, Ben,' Amy cried as Jack crumpled to his knees.

　　　　*　　　　*　　　　*

'The doctor's with Mr Barnes. His family are in the apartment with him, ma'am. Oh, and the South Wales police are on the line,' a constable informed Amy when she and Ben returned to the incident room after leaving Patrick and the forensic team in the garage.

'Put the call through to the small office,' Ben ordered.

'And ask Michael Barnes to come down here. We need to interview him again,' Amy added before following Ben.

　　　　*　　　　*　　　　*

The phone was ringing when Ben walked in. The male voice on the end of the line had a heavy Welsh accent. 'Am I talking to Sergeant Ben Miller?'

'Speaking.'

'Constable Tom Edwards. You

131

wanted to know about the fire at Castle Owens.'

'Jack Barnes's house,' Ben checked.

'That's the one. It happened two years ago?'

'Yes. Was it caused by faulty electrical wiring?'

'The wiring that connected the pump to the boiler was the wrong grade. Suitable for lighting, not power circuits.'

'The builder was responsible?'

'Jack Barnes called Tad Moore in to renovate the place. Tad swore he'd used the right cable, but the jury didn't believe him. He was found guilty and fined.'

Ben thought he detected scepticism in Tom's voice. 'Did you believe him?'

'I've known Tad twenty years. I trusted him to rewire my mam's house, but Mam's wiring was inspected after completion. A small repair like the one in Castle Owens wasn't. Then again, Tad admitted he'd only done a temporary job. He said he intended to return the next day to finish it. That's what settled it for the jury. They decided he'd botched it. He paid his fine but was ruined. Went bankrupt. No one would employ him to tie up their roses afterwards, let alone rewire a house.'

'Jack Barnes's wife—'

'Jodie. Nice girl. Grew up in the village. She went to school with my daughter.'

'What was the cause of death?'

'Fire. Pathologist couldn't determine more. Wasn't enough left for a post mortem. They identified her from dental records. She was found on the living-room sofa. Pathologist thought she'd fallen asleep, which would explain why she didn't hear the fire alarms. It was a tragedy. She was six months pregnant. If you don't mind me asking, why are you looking into this now?'

'Jack Barnes's second wife has been murdered. She was five months pregnant.'

'I don't like coincidences. But Jack Barnes was out of the country—in America when Jodie died.'

Ben thought it an odd remark for a police officer to make. 'Were there rumours?'

'There are always rumours when someone young dies unexpectedly. Jodie had just moved into the castle by herself. Some people thought it strange, given she was six months pregnant. They thought a man would want to be with his wife, especially as there was work to be done and builders to contend with. Jodie said that Jack was on a business trip but would join her later.'

'He didn't?'

'He came quickly enough after he was told she was dead. You know what gossips are.'

'Tell me,' Ben prompted.

'They thought a rich, important man like Jack Barnes, used to getting his own way, wanted to dump pregnant Jodie in the country near her family—somewhere she wouldn't be able to see him playing around.'

'Castle Owens was supposed to be a weekend place, wasn't it?'

'Weekend place? It was a castle, and Jack Barnes was throwing money at it.'

Ben recalled Leila talking about Jack's wandering eye, but he also remembered the look of anguish on Jack's face when he'd seen Zee's body. That grief was real. He'd stake his career on it.

'Who reported the fire?'

'A farmer who lived a mile away. He went to check on a calf before going to bed, saw the flames and called the fire brigade. They got there too late for Jodie. There were only the stone walls of the place left. I was surprised they found her body. I would never have recognised it as human.'

'Thank you.' Ben tried to end the call.

'Before you go, Jack Barnes never rebuilt the castle. It was insured. He took the money but left the ruins. I heard the council asked him to clear the site. There's no sign of any work starting. You know anything about it?'

'Nothing.'

'If you have suspicions about Jodie Barnes's death I could call the pathologist. Old Howell wrote the report. He's retired. In fact, they brought him out to look at poor Jodie because Evans, the regular pathologist was on holiday—'

'I have no suspicions,' Ben interrupted. 'Just wanted to confirm that Jack Barnes's first wife's death was an accident.'

'Had to be. No one else was around. Lonely spot, Castle Owens.'

'Thank you for your help, Constable Edwards.'

'If you need any more information . . .'

'I'll contact you. Goodbye.' Ben replaced the receiver.

'Problem?' Amy asked.

'I'm not sure.'

'Jodie Barnes's death?'

'What we'd been told. She died alone in a fire in a castle that Jack was renovating. Faulty wiring. The electrician was blamed and fined. There wasn't enough left of her to carry out a full post mortem.'

'Cause of death?'

'To quote Constable Edwards, "Fire", but the pathologist who examined her remains was old and retired.'

'Why was he trusted to examine the remains?'

'The regular pathologist was on holiday.'

Amy looked up at a knock on the door. 'Enter.'

'Michael Barnes is here, ma'am.'

'Show him in, Constable.'

'Hold him a moment, Constable,' David Reece contradicted. He walked in and closed the door behind him. 'We found a bloodstained shirt in Ted Levett's linen bin. We've sent it to the lab, but a technician said the stains matched those on the knives found in the chefs' apartment.'

'The knives were cleaned on the shirt?' Amy asked.

'Wiped more than cleaned, according to him, and after the shirt had been worn. Dirt stains confirm it. Do you want me to arrest Ted Levett?'

CHAPTER TWENTY-TWO

Amy thought for a moment. 'Yes, arrest him, but hold Ted here. I'll interview him as soon as I can, and don't allow Damian Clark to leave the building.'

'No, ma'am.'

'Very neat. Ted kills Zee with Bruno's knives, cleans the blood on his shirt and drops it into his linen bin for us to find. Then returns the knives to Bruno's apartment, unexpectedly finds him at home and kills him because Bruno's a witness.' David looked at Amy. 'Someone is trying to implicate Ted as the murderer.'

'Someone a touch heavy-handed and obvious. Show Michael in.'

*   *   *

'After seeing Jack, I'll do whatever I can to help bring the bastard who killed Zee to justice,' Michael said vehemently.

'I'd appreciate your co-operation after your attitude earlier,' Amy said.

Michael moved uneasily. 'I didn't know then that Zee had been murdered, or that Jack had been sent her heart.'

'You didn't like Zee.' Amy had stated a fact, not asked a question.

'At first I thought she'd caught Jack on the rebound after Jodie's death,' Michael agreed. 'But after seeing how happy she made Jack, I made an effort to get to know her.'

'Did Zee improve on acquaintance?' Ben watched Michael's face.

'She wasn't the obvious choice for Jack,' Michael was cautious. 'Jodie was a college lecturer; Zee was a waitress. She was kind, though, and helped Jack relax. He's always worked too hard.'

Amy recalled Leila's insistence that Zee was mercenary. 'You weren't worried about the money Jack was spending on her?'

Michael shrugged. 'It's Jack's money.'

'You live rent-free?' Amy checked.

'Only because Jack refuses to take rent from us. He owns the building and converted it to give the family a London base. He's protective towards Mamie and thought she'd feel more secure with her brothers as well as her sister around.'

'It doesn't bother you, accepting your brother's charity?' Ben persevered.

'Jack's rich, but money's never been as important to him as running a successful business. We live rent-free, but Jack doesn't pay us an allowance, as he does Mamie and Leila.'

'How much does he pay them?' Ben's pen was poised over his notebook.

'You'd have to ask them or Jack.'

'You live on what you make from your art?' Amy queried.

'Last year I made less than two thousand pounds from sales to galleries and spent five thousand on materials. Please treat this as confidential. It could ruin my reputation as a serious artist if it got out. I illustrate advertisements, comic books and graphic novels. One a week brings in around fifty to sixty thousand a year.'

'Nice work if you can get it,' Ben commented.

'I don't need my brother's money,' Michael agreed.

'And your sisters?'

'Our father left money in trust for Mamie. Leila gave up nursing to care for her when our parents were killed. I have no idea how much is in the trust. I've never asked. Jack supplements it. I asked him if he wanted me to contribute. He didn't.'

'Do you know if your brother has made a will?' Amy saw Michael hesitate. 'I'm asking you because I'd rather not press Jack at the moment.'

'Before he married Jodie, I was executor and a beneficiary along with Leila and Mamie. After he married, he changed his will in Jodie's favour. When she died, he reverted to his original will, which he changed again when he married Zee. His last will favoured Zee and the child she was carrying.'

Amy closed the interview. 'Thank you, Mr Barnes.'

*   *   *

Ted had been cautioned and was under guard in his apartment. Damian was at the porter's desk. Skinny, pale-faced, he looked like a man who seldom ventured out into fresh air. He glanced at the photograph of Ted's shirt that Amy was showing him.

'Ted wore it the day before yesterday.'

'Are you sure?' Ben questioned.

'Positive,' Damian retorted. 'The guy only has five shirts and he bought three of those from the charity shop after he started work here. There's blood on it.'

'We noticed,' Ben said dryly.

'Surely you can't think . . .'

'What, Mr Clark?' Amy asked.

'Ted worshipped Mrs Barnes. If it hadn't been for her persuading Mr Barnes to give Ted a job and flat, he'd be in a hostel, or living rough.'

'You like Ted?'

'Not when I first met him. I'd seen him selling *The Big Issue*. I thought Mrs Barnes had picked him up because she felt sorry for him. The way some people take in stray dogs. Ted knew what I thought of him because I wasn't very welcoming, but he wasn't afraid of hard work. He took on the dirty jobs from his first day: collecting the rubbish, putting out the bins, checking the chemicals in the pool, and if I want an hour or two off, he's always willing to cover for me.'

'You're trying to tell us Ted Levett is a nice man who isn't capable of murder.'

'I'm a writer, Sergeant Miller. I study people,' Damian said pompously. 'I believe we're all capable of murder if we're threatened, but there's no way Ted Levett killed Mrs Barnes. He thought too much of her.'

'Thank you,' Amy ended the interview.

'Do you want to interview Ted Levett?' Ben asked Amy.

'Not before I interview Mamie Barnes.'

'Why Mamie?'

'I've been told people with Down's Syndrome don't lie. I thought I'd test the theory.'

CHAPTER TWENTY-THREE

The constable on duty outside the penthouse opened the door when Amy and Ben approached.

Irene Conway met them in the hall. 'Michael, Leila and Jack's secretary, Alice, are with Jack in the den. Mamie's in the living room. Anni went to the gallery.'

Amy entered the living room. Mamie was sitting on a sofa holding a rose and Valentine card.

'Hello, Mamie.'

'You know my name?'

'I'm Amy Stuart, this is Ben Miller. We're police officers.'

'You're here because someone did something bad to Zee, aren't you, Amy?'

Amy hesitated, unsure what Mamie had been told.

'Zee gave me these.' Mamie held up the card and rose.

'They're lovely, Mamie.'

'Please sit down.' Mamie had been taught to play the hostess.

Amy and Ben sat on a sofa opposite Mamie.

'Is Zee dead?'

'What did your brothers and sister tell you?' Amy asked cautiously.

'That Zee's in heaven and I won't see her any more.'

'That's right, Mamie,' Amy answered.

'I liked Zee.' Mamie paused. 'Now Jack hasn't a wife again. Jodie, his first wife, was nice like Zee. She used to take me to the park.' Mamie's eyes filled with tears. 'She died.' Mamie fumbled beneath her blouse. 'Jodie gave me something for "a borrow", but I wasn't able to give it back. You're the police. I should give it to you.'

'Not if Jodie wanted you to have it, Mamie.'

'It's gold.' Mamie pulled a pendant from her collar.

'That's lovely, Mamie.' Amy admired the antique embossed locket.

'There's a secret inside. Jodie showed me.' Mamie's voice rose. 'I tried to give it back, but Leila said there was no time and Jodie wanted me to have it and—'

'Don't get upset, Mamie,' Amy tried to distract her. 'Can you show me the secret?'

Mamie flicked the catch on the

locket. It opened and a square of film fell out. Mamie picked it up and held it carefully by the edges. 'It's a picture of my nephew, taken before he was born,' Mamie said proudly. Her bottom lip trembled. 'Only he wasn't born. He was in Jodie's tummy when she died.'

'When did Jodie give you this, Mamie?' Amy took the film and handed it to Ben.

'When we saw her in Wales.' Mamie clamped her hands over her mouth. 'Leila made me promise never to tell anyone. I knew we were in Wales because I read the signs when we went over the big bridge. When we reached the castle, Jodie told me we were in Wales.'

'How long did you spend with Jodie, Mamie?' Ben asked.

'Part of a day. Jodie made us lunch. That's when she gave me the locket for "a borrow". After we'd eaten, Jodie fainted.'

'What happened then, Mamie?'

Amy prompted.

'Leila lifted Jodie on the sofa and sent me to the car. I waited a long time. When Leila came out of the castle I told her about the locket. That's when she said Jodie wanted me to keep it. I tried telling Leila that Jodie only gave it to me for "a borrow", but Leila got cross and told me to shut up about the locket. Then Leila drove back to the hotel in Cornwall. After our holiday, Leila said Jodie had died and I wasn't to upset Jack by talking about her. I wanted to tell Jack about the locket, but I was afraid he'd be angry with me, like Leila. Then Jack met Zee.' Mamie's voice dropped to a whisper. 'Now she's dead too.'

Leila walked in with Jack, Michael and Alice.

'I thought I heard Mamie talking,' Leila reproached Amy. 'You can't interview her. I'm her guardian and I won't allow it. She left the building before Zee this morning. She knows nothing—'

'But she does know something about Jodie,' Ben said.

'Jodie?' Jack looked at Mamie in bewilderment.

'I'm sorry, Leila. I didn't mean to tell them,' Mamie pleaded.

'Mamie doesn't know what she's saying,' Leila argued. 'She has no sense of time, people or places.'

'On the contrary, Miss Barnes. We've found Mamie helpful and lucid,' Ben contradicted.

'Mamie, is that Jodie's locket?' Jack drew near his sister and examined it.

'Jodie gave it to me for "a borrow", Jack.'

'Jodie would never have given you that.' Jack paled. His eyes darkened.

'Only for "a borrow".' Mamie began to cry.

Jack crouched down in front of Mamie. 'I'm not angry with you, but I want to know when Jodie gave you this. I thought she was wearing it when she died.'

'She gave it to me in Wales.'

'You were in Wales with Jodie?' Jack asked Leila.

'Mamie will say anything, Jack. You know what she's like . . . '

'Mamie doesn't lie,' Jack countered. 'When did you see Jodie in Wales, Mamie?'

'When Leila drove us there from Cornwall—'

'That's enough, Mamie . . . '

'I've never hit a woman, Leila, but if you don't shut up I will,' Jack threatened.

'You're cross with me,' Mamie gulped between sobs.

Jack slipped his arm around his younger sister's shoulders. 'I'm not cross with you, Mamie. Tell me about your trip to Wales.'

'Leila and me left the hotel early so we could eat lunch with Jodie. Jodie was nice, like she always was. Then she was ill and Leila sent me to the car. That was after Jodie gave me the locket. I tried to give it back, Jack . . . I tried . . .'

Jack patted Mamie's shoulders but watched Leila. 'You never told me you visited Jodie in Wales, Leila.'

'Because I knew you'd be suspicious. You thought we didn't get on.'

'You were the reason Jodie wanted a retreat in Wales.'

'She wanted to get away from your womanising,' Leila snapped.

'What womanising?' Michael was clearly mystified.

Leila ignored Michael. 'You and Zee were a bloody disgrace, Jack. I don't know why you bothered to marry her. The way you carry on with your secretary and Zee with Ted. Her blood was all over his shirt . . .'

'Who told you Zee's blood was on Ted's shirt, Leila?' Ben interrupted.

Her cheeks turned red. 'One of the police constables.'

'Police officers have faults, but a

152

loose mouth is trained out of them,' Amy stated.

'It's obvious. Ted's the only one who could have killed Zee.' Leila's voice grew shrill. 'He had the master key code. He could move around the building . . . '

'We need to interview you, Miss Barnes. Alone,' Amy said firmly. 'Sergeant Miller, please escort Miss Leila Barnes downstairs and call for a car to take her to the station.'

Before Ben could hustle Leila to the door, Jack stepped between them.

'Jodie, Zee and Bruno,' Jack challenged. '*You* killed them!'

Leila gazed at him, but not for long. She realised she'd said too much to continue protesting her innocence. 'Bruno was a mistake. I thought he was working. But he saw me returning the knives. As for Jodie and Zee, I did you a favour, Jack. They were tramps. You might have been blind to the way Zee carried on with Ted, but I wasn't.'

'Ted and Zee were only friends,' Michael broke in.

'No they weren't. Couldn't you see what Ted was up to? Sleeping with Zee. Worming his way into everyone's affections until you all preferred Ted to me. Never mind what I've done for you boys, as well as Mamie. Giving up my life and my career to care for her. And you?' Leila demanded of Jack. 'What would you have done once you became a father? Would you still have paid me an allowance to look after Mamie?'

'Of course . . .'

'There's no, "of course". You were besotted with the idea of becoming a father. You would have tossed Mamie and me aside. That's why Jodie and Zee had to go.'

'Damn you, Leila. I saw Zee's body. Saw what you did to her . . . ' Jack slumped on a chair. Michael went to him.

Ben motioned to Irene. 'Ask the constable outside to come in and cuff Miss Barnes.'

Leila screamed hysterically as handcuffs were snapped on to her wrists. 'Everything I did, I did for you boys and Mamie. Promise me you'll look after her, Jack? Promise me . . . '

'Jack doesn't have to promise you anything, Leila,' Michael answered as Ben and the constable escorted her to the door. 'As for Mamie, me and Jack, we'll look after one another.'

A heavy silence, punctuated by Mamie's quiet sobs, settled over the room after Leila had left with Ben and the constable.

When Amy could stand the tension no longer, she said, 'I'm so sorry, Mr Barnes.'

Jack took Mamie into his arms. She buried her head in his shoulder. He looked over her head at Amy. 'Thank you, Inspector Stuart. You did your job and did it well.'

Too close to tears to speak, Amy nodded. She left the apartment, closed the door quietly behind her and joined the others at the lift.